DORIAN'S QUARTERBACK

Mary Taylor

www.blackstonefinn.com

CONTENTS

Title Page

Copyright

Dedication

Epigraph

Preface

PART 1: CHILDHOOD IMPRINTS   1

DINOSAURS & SNOW ANGELS   3

WE ARE   23

SPAGHETTI & BULLIES   34

MIDOL & TIGER BEAT   60

PART 2: TEENAGE IMPRINTS   67

FOUND & LOST   68

HIGHWAY TO HELL   93

WHAT'S IN A NAME?   106

COLD DUCK   145

DEATH AT 14   154

GIVING THANKS   177

WHITMAN & GINSBERG   200

LONDON BOY   204

GREASE TRAPS FOR DANTE 241

LETTERS, LETTERS, LETTERS 255

DORIAN'S QUARTERBACK 272

TOBY'S FIRST CHRISTMAS 289

... 317

Discussion Questions 319

Emotional Imprints Series 321

Praise For Dorian's Quarterback 323

Praise For Dinosaurs & Snow Angels 325

Praise For Pitch, Yaw & Roll 327

Acknowledgements 329

About The Author 331

PREFACE

2020 was a wake-up call for the world. My decision to self-publish was a direct result of the events of that year.

In 2021, I cut my teeth on *Dinosaurs & Snow Angels*; *Pitch, Yaw & Roll*; and *The Grand Fascination*. This helped me discover my velocity; set a release cadence; have early reader feedback; and provided bite-size, shorter reads for busy people.

At the end of 2021, the revised stories and structure along with additional chapters and new characters conspired to become *Dorian's Quarterback*, the novel.

Dorian's Quarterback, spans from Beth's 1970s childhood to her 16th year when she falls hard for Toby, and first encounters a mysterious disease in 1981.

As a concept, the *Emotional Imprints Series* flowed from my own struggles and search around questions of identity, love, belonging and faith. I began serious excavation of my emotional imprints since becoming sober in 2015.

Like the main character, I have always been a sensitive, curious, keen observer. I am fascinated by the questions of what shapes a life, what makes a person who they are? Are one's emotional imprints ever truly knowable? If they can be identified and understood, can a person change the course of their life, or will they be forever subconsciously chained to those imprints of the past?

In 2022, The Emotional Imprints Series will continue with a second novel, wherein Beth will face increasingly complex challenges around questions of identity, love, sexuality, gender, faith and belonging.

~ Mary Taylor, December 21, 2021
Blackstonefinn.com

PART 1: CHILDHOOD IMPRINTS

1970s

DINOSAURS & SNOW ANGELS

Three days past Christmas, the snow begins to fall again. I search for my mother in our cavernous, cold house. My oldest brother William Jr., his wife Hope, and their son Little Will left that morning. Dad was back at work. Mom was somewhere, and I was cold and searching for her.

The twelve-foot tree still in the sunroom, but now, no colorful presents beneath it, just dry needles and fallen tinsel.

My nephew Little Will was only three years younger and more of a brother to me than my real brothers ever were.

During the holidays, we transformed this mansion into our magical playground:

In the wine cellar we were spies searching for top secret information hidden in dusty secret places.

In the living room, the space underneath the long couch was our escape tunnel from East to West Berlin. We were spies with rug burn on our knees.

In the ballroom, we were Batman and Robin and Dad's WWII field phone became our Bat-phone.

The original owners custom-built the house in the 1920s with a third floor for their cooks and maids. A private stairway from the third floor was the perfect hiding place to spy on whatever was happening in the kitchen.

Different from the rest of the house, the walls were the color of pistachio ice cream, the wooden steps were painted that same color with shiny, black rubber strips nailed over them instead of carpet.

I search for her in the kitchen.

"Mom?"

She is not there either.

Just a few nights before that same kitchen was full of warm bread smells and laughter.

Hiding in that pistachio-green stairway, Little Will and I played "Dinosaur" a game where everyone in the family was a Dinosaur by number.

"Dinosaur 1 is at the kitchen table," I said.

"Where's Dinosaur 2? Let me looooook!"

"Shhh," I say, "they'll hear us."

Dinosaur 2 is William Jr., Little Will's dad, my oldest brother. He was not there.

We strain to hear the table of women. All the women of the family are in the kitchen except for me.

I was not yet a woman, but rather just a girl, a skinny colt-legged tomboy with long hair and my father's square fingers. I couldn't wait to be all grown-up like my sister Lydia and my sister-in-law Hope.

My nineteen-year-old sister Lydia home from college for winter break shares that she has decided that she wants to major in Russian studies. She had always been excellent at languages and lived in France for a year in upper school.

"Lydia, your father is paying for you to get an education for your future, how will Russian be of any use?"

"I was thinking maybe D.C., you know, maybe intelligence," Lydia says.

"I was stationed in Washington, D.C. during the war and I could have gone to MIT after, but I went to work instead."

Lydia rolled her eyes, "I know mom, you have told that story a thousand times."

"Well, Hope and Kate may not have heard it. I had been offered a full scholarship, and was the only woman they admitted for a master's degree in engineering. I would have gone on to be a civil engineer, but I chose to get a job instead, and that's where I met your father."

Mother wearing her big, puffy, stove mittens, pulls out fresh loaves of bread from the oven. Powdered loaves raised high and golden they spill over their pans.

She sets them lovingly on the cooling racks next to the stove. Like many women of her generation, she was expected to marry and raise a family.

"How did you and Mr. Lawrence meet?" Hope asked.

Mom giggled like the young woman she once was and said,

"We met at a summer company picnic. Mind you, I was still pretty new to the job, and walking by this group of loud, arrogant men who were drinking beers - "

"Oh no, here we go," Lydia said.

"Lydia, hush. Well, I heard this one man say the darndest thing, he said, 'Fellas, there's *nothing worse* than a Pembroker or a W.A.C.'"

She took off her oven mitts, and placed linen napkins in front of each of the three women.

"Well, I stopped. Turned to him and said, 'Sir, I don't know who you are, but I will have you know I graduated from Pembroke *and* I proudly served in the Women's Army Corps!'"

Hope laughed, "Then what happened?"

"I got more potato salad," she laughed, "He took me on a lovely date, we were crazy for each other, of course. Within three months he asked my father's permission for my hand in marriage. He proposed and we were married within a year."

"And then William Junior appeared on the scene soon after," Lydia chuckled.

"Lydia," mom scolded, "why do you imply such things? I was a virgin until my wedding night, and your father is the only man I have ever loved."

"That's romantic," Kate said almost too quiet for us eavesdropping spies to hear.

"Yes, quite," mom said, "and he was so handsome with that jet-black hair and those blue eyes."

"Things are changing now mom, women want careers outside the home," Lydia said.

"My mother, your grandmother, did not even have the right to vote. She sold encyclopedias door-to-door to pay for her college education."

"She told me that she was forced to quit her job when she got married," Lydia said.

"Forced to?" Kate asked.

"Yes," Lydia continued, "Grandma taught Spanish after she graduated from college, and back then it was against the law for married women to teach. Wasn't that it mom?"

"Yes," mom said as she smoothed her apron. "You girls are very lucky to have many more opportunities than your grandmothers ever had."

Years later in the rubble of the big-truth, mother would confide in me just how much the "what ifs" had haunted her. *Wasted potential, it's the curse of being born at the wrong time.*

The women looked at each other in silence for a long time. So quiet, I could hear Little Will breathing. I was sure we'd get caught spying.

"So I guess I'm the only woman of the family who never went to college," Hope said in a loud voice.

Hope, my sister-in-law, has her back to us secret spies hiding in the stairway. The kitchen chair dwarfs under her large curvaceous body.

Lydia speaks some Russian words in a low tone of voice. She animates a joke that I cannot understand but Hope does.

Hope's high-pitched laugh is full and round like the rich sound of the brass handbells played every year at my school's Christmas Vespers.

She laughs with her whole body. Head back, her shoulders shake up and down. She tilts back in her chair as if she needs more room for all that joy inside her.

My mother with her proper lipstick smile is the conductor of the kitchen, the perfect hostess. She listens to these women, smiling with the occasional girlish giggle. A measured laugh just big enough, but never "unladylike".

And then there is Kate, tall, quiet, her thin body reed-like, she sits angled in her chair, across the table from Lydia. Her legs crossed with a flat palm hidden between her thighs. Kate is the wife of my other brother George who was fourteen when I was born. Brilliant George had a mean-streak wider than his perfect Ivy League lettered life would ever let on. Like him, Kate will be forever holding everything inside.

It is Hope's laughter, Hope's lifeforce that fills the kitchen that night with warmth and joy. Over thick slices of warm bread and butter, my sister, Mom and Kate can't help but laugh and smile for Hope's happiness is contagious.

Little Will and I hiding on the back stairs now convinced we are unseen and unheard as we witness these women through the small crack in the door ajar.

"Let me see," Little Will whispers "what are they laughing about?"

His small hand reaches for the glass doorknob. I move over to sit down on the stairs. His brown corduroys bunched and baggy, his belt over a missed belt loop, and his socks half-off from our earlier escape from East Berlin through the secret tunnel under the couch.

After Little Will was put to bed, me in my sock feet padded quietly back towards the kitchen. Not from the back stairs, but slow, through the main hallway. They were drinking tea now, my sister holding a thick handmade blue mug she made in her ceramics class.

I walked in on some adult talk: something about Hope's father, whom they called "Pop", not allowing any "bastards" to come into his family. Something about Little Will being a mistake.

When they saw me the room got quiet real fast.

I sat up on my sister's lap and reached for a slice of the fresh bread. I spread the butter on thick and slow, the question burning in my mind slipped out.

"What's a bastard?"

My sister cleared her throat behind me choking down a laugh.

"Nothing," Mom said. "It's nothing."

"It's a child born out of wedlock," Hope said.

"*Conceived* out of wedlock," Lydia said.

"Was Little Will a bastard?"

"No, honey, he wasn't," Hope said.

My mother's back to me, she's doing something at the stove. Kate sips her tea without making a sound.

Smells of bread, the butter soft on my knife, the room got heavy with quiet.

I took a bite wondering if I should ask the question. I was always asking questions, and much of the time got in a lot of trouble for it.

My face got hot as I chewed the delicious bread, swallowed, then asked,

"Was he a mistake?"

"No," Hope said, "he wasn't."

My sister patted her hands hard on my hips and bounced me up and down on her knees.

"But *you* were," she said in a sing-songy voice.

My mother jumped. "*Lydia*, that's enough."

Then turning to me her face hard, "Young lady, you ask too many questions!"

I looked over at Hope. Her eyes reaching for mine. Her lips curved in a sad closed half-smile. I recognized Hope then as the only truth in the room.

"Is the baklava cool enough now?" Kate asked.

My mother welcomed the diversion, and put a pan of sticky flakey pastry on the table,

"Yes Kate, would you please cut that for us?"

Mom handed Kate a fancy knife specifically for cutting pastry without damaging the pan.

I watched Kate's steady, quiet hand cut diagonal lines into small, sweet triangles.

Mistake?

Bastard?

Something about Pop not wanting her to have it. No Little Will? There was a possibility that he might not have been? I could not imagine life without him. He was the brother to me that mine never were.

I jumped off my sister's lap, and went into the living room, to do something I did not like to do: Math.

I knew it took nine months to make a baby. I knew when he was born, and I knew when Hope and my brother got married. With a pencil and paper I got my answer: they made him before they got married.

Seeing those numbers penciled-out on paper the mysterious concept of sex became real to me in a way it hadn't before. I realized what my brother and Hope did together made Little Will, and they made him before they got married.

My body tingled with the delicious thrill that I discovered a secret. Something that had been too taboo to discuss in front of me. Something mom did not want me to know.

We had some sex education at school in the form of "It's what mommy and daddy do when they love each other" and Judy Blume's *Are You There God? It's Me, Margaret*. And then there were the ink anatomy diagrams that made sex look as gross as the black lung images they showed to warn us about the dangers of smoking.

Being an all-girls progressive school, our teacher did her best to be candid and forthcoming, but sometimes even she would blush at our questions and comments. Like when Janey announced that boys and girls are not really that different at all because she tried to pee standing up like her brother does and it "kinda works."

Ms. Gillhern said that was fine to do at home, but admonished her to not try that in the school bathrooms. This only resulted in further nervous whispers and giggles.

This new information about Little Will was different. It had the heavy feelings of responsibility and seriousness, curiosity and fear all bundled together. More powerful than what I had heard at school or even saw in the books my sister brought back from France. In the 1970s there was no talk of "safe sex" yet, and birth control was not openly discussed either. Sex was still such a mystery.

Having much older siblings had created a longing to discover the secrets and mysteries of growing-up from an early age, but now I had a new feeling: a profound sense of fear.

Fear.

And doubt.

That night when Hope tucked me in under my winter flannel sheets and down comforter, she placed her hand on my head and ran her fingers slow across my scalp and through my long hair. My whole body immediately relaxed at her touch.

"Was Little Will a mistake?" I asked.

"No," Hope said gently, "I told you he wasn't."

"But you weren't married...when you made him?"

"That's right," Hope said, "your brother and I were so much in love we couldn't wait."

Her voice was soft and kind. I knew in that moment I could ask her anything.

"But Pop told you not to have him?"

"Yes," she said, "he forbid me to have a child at my age. I had just turned seventeen, and that was too young. I was supposed to go on to college, so my parents arranged for me to go to Paris to... to..."

The light from the hallway on Hope's face, her eyes got shiny.

"...but then your brother and I went to talk to your father. We were both terrified. He sat us down and asked us if we loved each other. We said yes, and he was kind and supportive. He gave us his blessing and told us that if we wanted to get married he would help us any way he could. Your father was wonderful to us. He still is."

"I'm glad you got married," I said, "I can't imagine life without you or Little Will."

With her hand still on my head, she turned away and bent her cheek towards her shoulder, wiping her tears.

Then, smiling big, her teeth perfectly straight and beautiful she said,

"Listen, have you ever made snow angels?"

"I don't think so," I said.

"That's what we are going to do tomorrow. You and Little Will and I are going to make snow angels out on the boulevard."

Her hand bigger and warmer than my mom's. Soft and yielding yet firm. I started to drift-off to dreams of Christopher Robin and Pooh making snow angels in the Hundred Acre Wood.

And now three days past Christmas, Hope's gone. They're all gone. The living room is so much bigger now, empty with memories. The same living room where just the day before Little Will and I played catch with a gold damask pillow from the couch. *I'm gonna be like Joe Namath, and play football!*

Remembering Little Will's challenge, *betcha can't walk on your hands*, I launch into a handstand, walk six feet on my hands and then cart-wheel though the grey light of afternoon snow-fall and soft shadows.

Giggles and Legos, and headstands on pillows. Every day for that whole week Little Will and I created magical worlds in which we would play and laugh until that time mom declared,

"Nap time! You two are overtired. Time to go lie down!"

"But mom it's not even lunchtime!"

"You two are too excited and are being too silly, you must be overtired. I will call you both when lunch is ready."

And we were sent off to our rooms as if being punished with a "time out" which was a new par-enting technique in the '70s.

Instead of "the strap" which was used on gen-erations before, a child would be sent to their room to think about what they had done and then respond accordingly. We were not being punished for anything wrong officially and yet we were. I sat on my pink bedspread with my constant companions of Leo, Teddy, Rupert and Peter Rabbit and the shame seeped in.

It was as if our happiness made her unhappy. And too much happiness expressed upset mom.

This would be one of the marks, a part of that larger imprint that said *there were negative conse-quences for too much happiness.*

I told Peter Rabbit, "I'd better tone it down a bit. I need to set a good example for Little Will, he's just a baby."

Sitting in my pink and white bedroom on my bed I shared with stuffed animals, I thought about Hope. She never scolded us for being silly or happy or laughing too much.

I wanted to go back in time. Such a strange thing is time. Seemingly shorter and faster when Hope and Little Will were around. Always longer before and after their visits.

The house swallows me. I walk slow up the long, wide carpeted staircase. Tall cathedral-like stained-glass windows tower over the landing. Gray winter light throws soft colors on the oak wainscoting and gold Berber carpet.

My small hand slides up the banister that just yesterday, Little Will and I were sliding down. Our game was to go as fast as you could and stop yourself just before your tailbone would hit that large wooden acorn at the bottom using our hands as breaks. The banister cools under my cold hand as I walk up the stairs.

"Mom, where are you?"

I turn at the landing and take the last four stairs. The door to my parent's master bedroom is closed.

I knock and hear a distant 'come in'.

The large quiet fills the largest bedroom of the house. My parent's master bedroom runs the length of the house complete with huge bath and separate his and her wardrobe rooms for dressing.

Mother stands over by the bay window in her burgundy wool suit, complete with stockings and dressy heels. She always looks nice. I walk up next to her. Her lipstick the same burgundy red to match her wool suit.

She is cleaning up the Christmas wrapping. The large metal radiator between her and the bay window, I put my hands on the grey marble slab top. It is warm, the radiator alive with the hiss of steam and tapping metal sounds.

The greens, golds, whites, and reds of ribbon are colorful snakes that will have to wait for next year to escape. She wraps them around their individual cardboard cylinders and lays them down in a box side by side. Green, Gold, White, and Red.

"Oh, dear, the tags are all mixed up," she said.

"I'm sorry," I said.

The mess was my fault but I didn't want to tell her why. Christmas eve, father had asked me to wrap a special small box, *Would you wrap this for me? It's for your mother, and you always wrap presents much prettier than I can.* And so, I happily wrapped the gift, but I had been in a hurry and left a mess looking for the last tag with a snowman and cheerful birds that carry pretty ribbons in their beaks. Mom loved the ruby pendant so much and she commented on how beautifully he'd wrapped it. Dad winked at me and so it was our little secret that I had wrapped it for him.

The heat of the radiator underneath my hands and elbows. I lean into the warmth. My skinny legs, my pelvis. Even my bones are cold, my chest empty.

Mom picks up the orphaned papers - ones that were cut too small or shaped too awkward to wrap a gift. She flattens them into a neat stack and then rolls them up and puts them in ribbon bag.

"Waste not, want not," she says.

"Mom?"

"Yes dear?"

"Was I...was I a mistake?"

Her hands stop moving. Her brown eyes flat on mine for just a second, then back to the little rectangle tags.

Santas placed with Santas and Candy Canes with Candy Canes.

"Your father and I always wanted four children," she said, "two boys and two girls, and that's what God gave us."

"But why am I *so* much younger than Lydia and George and William Jr.?"

"We had you a few years later," she said, "that's all."

The side of my mom's face, intent on what she is doing. Her hair a soft brown that curled at the bottom and a wave that went across her forehead. A classic beauty, like Katharine Hepburn or Lauren Bacall. My mother didn't smile like pretty women do because she didn't know she was pretty. Decades later after everything bad had settled, she would tell me that her parents always called her the 'smart' one and her sister was the 'pretty' one.

The warmth of the radiator under my palms and fingers. I wanted that warmth to engulf me. The warmth hugged me through the sleeves of my forest green school uniform sweater. The cold hollow ache of my chest pushing up now stuck in my throat. My face got hot; eyes stung.

"I miss Hope," I said.

"I know you do dear."

Mom stacked the name cards into their little cardboard cubbyholes.

Santas with Santas. Waiting till next year.

"But, I'm...I'm sad, really sad," I said.

The ribbons and bows blurred, green, red and gold prisms in my eyes.

"You'll feel better tomorrow," she said, "and next week when you're back in school, you'll be so busy you'll forget they were here."

I wipe my eyes and look out at the snow on the trees. The wide empty boulevard. No one was making snow angels now.

"I don't want to forget," I said quietly.

I wanted more.

More laughter and magical adventures with Little Will.

More of Hope's big arms hugging me. Her laughter. Her comfort.

I wanted more dinosaurs, more snow angels.

I tried to understand what mom said. It didn't make sense to me, but it must be true if she said it: this pain in my chest and heavy sadness would go away once I got back to school.

I stood there too long. Wanting something she couldn't give to me. My toes cold in my shoes. I wished I could put my feet on the radiator too.

"Shouldn't you be reading? Didn't your school assign you a reading list for Christmas break?"

"Yes."

"Well, better hop to it young lady! We don't want to fall behind, do we?"

The paper organized. All the bundles of pretty colors were back in their clear plastic bags and cardboard boxes until next year.

Rolls of paper and boxes in her arms, Mom turned and walked away. I picked up as much as I could off the bay window and radiator and followed her out the bedroom, across the landing by the large stained-glass windows, and up into the pistachio-green staircase to the third floor.

I did not like the third floor there were boogeymen up there. The whole space gave me the creeps. The only time it felt safe was when Little Will was with me, and we would go up there to send secret messages and his stuffed tiger down the laundry chute.

Mom walked into the far back room that would overlook the cherry tree blossoms in April. Now it was covered with snow. Mom bent down slow. Elegant, she never ran her hose. She turned the small latch to open the elf door that went under the eaves, and she put the rolls of paper back there one by one.

Then she stepped aside for me to drop my bundles of ribbons and tags and bows. Of greens, blues, reds and golds.

It was dark and scary under the eaves. And smelled musty, dusty and dark. I laid the plastic bags down, backed out and mom gently closed the tiny door. The latch snapped shut. There was no latch on the inside.

My stomach clutched again. I hated going up there. I stayed close and followed mom back down the winding green stairway.

Her voice out in front of us, "I'm tired from all the excitement of the last week," she said, "I'm going to lie down for a nap."

She had wanted me to start on my reading homework, but she didn't bring it up again, so I followed her back into the master bedroom.

Mom was tired. She got tired a lot.

She took off her shoes, and with an audible sigh, she laid down on her half of the large four-poster bed. She pulled the crochet throw blanket up over her legs.

I took off my shoes on dad's side of the bed and carefully crawled over to her on my hands and knees slow so as not to disturb her.

She closed her eyes and crossed her hands over her chest like those Egyptian statues we saw pictures of in school. She looked asleep already. Or dead.

I curled-up fetal, perpendicular to her and carefully placed my head on her tummy. She did not object, so I relaxed a bit and listened to her heartbeat slow, soft, distant. Her breath shallow.

Her last rib, the floating rib, moved against the back of my head with each breath. I angled up a bit closer to feel her elbow against my upper back. My feet were still cold, I crossed them and pulled myself up into a ball as small as I could. Shaped and folded like when I was inside her womb.

Comfort in my ear, Mom's stomach sounded like the ocean sounds I would hear when snorkeling with Little Will in the summertime.

Gurgles and waves. Movement through water, food moving through acid. I close my eyes, and I try to fall asleep.

Maybe, just maybe, when I wake-up I won't miss Hope and Little Will so much.

WE ARE

Dad always drank his orange juice first thing in the morning.

Before coffee.

Before cereal.

Standing in his dark gray banker's suit, he surveyed the grassy well-manicured tree-lined boulevard though the big windows of our dining room. The reds and blues of the large thick oriental rug beneath his black, shiny shoes.

He drank his juice in a way that always made a sucking noise through his tight lips. He'd stand there drinking his juice and run his fingers though the loose change in his pocket.

His coins made a quick, sharp, jangly sound. That sound made my chest and gut tighten.

After his juice, he walked back across the dining room, through the swinging door, through the butler's pantry and into the kitchen.

I got our Fiestaware cereal bowls down from the cupboard and placed them across from each other on the kitchen table.

His favorite was orange, mine the pistachio green. He poured Quaker granola into his bowl, then spooned two heaps of sugar over the top with just a bit of milk.

My cereal was a choice between Special K or Grape Nuts with no extra sugar allowed.

"Ready for school today?"

Before I could answer, his eyes drifted past me. He'd chew and chew, crunchcrunchcrunch and rub his napkin between his thumb and forefinger until pieces of it would pill up and fall onto the brown Formica tabletop.

My Special-K got soggy. I poured in too much milk and wasn't eating it fast enough. My stomach hurt again.

Mom was not at the stove, nor in the pantry. There were many mornings since Lydia went to college when mom slept in late.

My dad's blue, blue eyes were sad and far away, although he was just three feet across the table from me.

My ribs clenched in on my stomach.

Third grade, and I was worried.

Jangling change, loud crunchy granola, dad grinding his napkin into powder ran his current of anxiety across the table and into me.

Most days, dad left for work before I left for

school, but today he would accompany me on my first time riding the city bus to school. It felt so grown up.

We walked the few blocks to the bus stop in silence. Alone together.

From the bus stop, I could see the large brick colonial. Dense, full hedges hugged the house all around. The corner of the sunroom with her tall windows that opened like French doors where we placed our twelve-foot Christmas tree every year.

But it was spring now, and the maple trees had just popped their bright, first-of-spring-green along the well-manicured boulevard.

It was a privileged childhood for certain, but I absorbed a deep sense of scarcity in that sea of privilege. Many of my classmates already knew they would be given a car of their choice when they turned sixteen and they were already planning what their debutante balls would look like and which boys they would ask to be their escort.

Even in second and third grade it was considered 'normal' for my classmates to safari in Africa and ski the Swiss Alps during the same winter vacation.

From that environment of privilege combined with my parent's childhood trauma and attitudes from the Great Depression and the War, I developed the warped perception that I was poor.

The poorest kid in a rich school and the only one with holes worn through the elbows of her wool uniform sweaters.

I could have a fleet of Mercedes or educated kids, I overheard dad say to his guests over cocktails, *I chose to have educated kids.*

Mom and dad were children of the Great Depression which taught them to value education and be extremely frugal. My mother's father lost everything when the market crashed. He owned a grocery store and allowed many of his customers a line of store credit. When the crash happened, no one could pay, and he lost his business. When my mother and her sister complained about eating oatmeal for weeks on end, my grandmother told her young daughters, *Be grateful your father did not jump out a window and kill himself.* The imprint of fear and abandonment.

My aunt and mother learned to not take anything for granted and never complain. Stoicism. Fear of scarcity was her trauma that shaped her to be frugal and hold all her fears inside. She made work and school top priorities and valued food as nutrition because she knew what it meant to literally go hungry for months.

Her father was a veteran of the First World War and started to wake his children every day with marching band music and set them to work. They grew vegetables and stored potatoes and winter squash in their cold cellar.

They made jam from summer blackberries and homemade bread, always wheat, never white because wheat had more nutritional value. To make ends meet, they allowed strangers to rent rooms in their house, which led to more trauma for the two young girls who did not have locks on their bedroom doors.

Dad's family was not hit as hard financially during the Great Depression although his trauma was just as deep if not greater. The sudden death of his father by heart attack forced him to become the 'man of the house' at only sixteen and care for his mother.

He fought in Europe after college, and mom served in Washington, DC. After the war, they both worked at the same bank where dad was a manager, and mom a bank teller. They met at a company picnic.

Dad often told the story of their first encounter just as much as mom did, but he emphasized her 'boldness' in telling him off. *One thing about your mother you can count on she's tough and not afraid to speak her mind.*

Dad was the congenial one who got along well with everyone. Their personalities complimented each other well.

Now several years and four children later, in the spring of 1974, the baby of the family and her dad waited.

Alone together at the bus stop.

I wore my school uniform skirt with a white Peter Pan collar shirt and my wool uniform blazer. Dad wore one of his grey suits with his grey Stetson hat, and his tan raincoat with the buttons that looked like round tasty caramels.

He held his chestnut-colored leather briefcase in front of him, his large square fingers wrapped around the worn leather handle.

I got his hands - wide paw hands with square boxy fingers. Dad shifted his briefcase to his left side, and with his right hand in his pocket, he ran his fingers through loose change. Moving his coins to make that quick, sharp, jangly sound that went right to my chest and stomach.

Did I remember my bus token?

I reached into the right pocket of my wool uniform blazer. I felt the thin, weightless disk about the size of nickel. I weaved that disk through my fingers inside the dark wool of my jacket pocket the same way dad's worried fingers ran through his change, but my actions were silent.

The front of the bus, a small box in the distance, moved towards us then stopped. Eight or so blocks and only three stops away. Dad punched the air straight out, bent his elbow and looked at his watch.

Finally, the bus reached us.

My father stepped back and I stepped up.

A puff of wind blew the dust up onto my face.

The bus doors folded open. I walked up the three steps. The driver smiled at me. I looked down and dropped my bus token into the change-eater slot.

A seat for two was open on the right about a third of the way back. I sat down and scooted in next to the window. My school uniform skirt went to my knees standing up, but sitting down it didn't cover me.

The seat was cold on the back of my legs. My legs were so skinny that even when I pushed my knees together tight, my green knee socks on my calves barely touched.

Colt legs mom always called them.

Dad dropped his real coins into the slot. A clink and a whirr with each coin dropped in. He turned and walked up the aisle.

As the bus started to move, he reached up and put his hand on the metal railing overhead.

He didn't look at me.

My palm patted the empty seat next to me, I opened my mouth, to say,

"Dad, right here."

I did say it, I think.

Or maybe, I didn't.

Because he did not seem to hear me or see me.

He sat down two rows ahead of me across the aisle.

Right.

There.

Next to an old lady with an orange paisley scarf covering her blue-grey hair.

My face got hot; my feet chilled cold. His salt and pepper hair cropped close, I could see it just below his hat, behind his ear. The angle of his strong square jaw. His eyes looking straight ahead.

At the next stop I pulled my canvas book bag up from the floor in front of me, and sat it on the empty seat next to me.

The empty seat where he should be.

Outside the bus window, I noticed two people jogging single file along the narrow dirt path that split the boulevard grass in two.

That same single-track path along the boulevard was where dad had taught me to ride my first grown-up bike without training wheels. A green Schwinn Sting-Ray with a banana seat and a flower-trimmed basket on the handlebars.

Sitting on the cold bus seat, my body recalled the somatic memory in my spine. The sensation at the second he let go, when instead of the bike wobbling to the ground as it had several times before, my balance worked and I didn't fall. *That's it, that's it!* his voice and clapping behind me as I rode farther away from him along the narrow dirt path.

Sitting on the bus, a smile came to my face remembering the shared feelings of pure joy and his pride at my simple accomplishment of riding a bike.

I looked over, and he was still just staring straight ahead. On my first city bus ride to school, I was no longer his daughter but just a person riding the same bus.

That tight feeling started again in my chest

and stomach. I closed my eyes and began to conjugate the French verbs we had just learned.

My face became hot with shame. I was not
good enough for him to sit with or even to ac-
knowledge.

Nerves churned my stomach and fluttered my
heart.

I started to conjugate the verb to be.

Je suis, I am.

Tu es, you are.

Il est, he is.

Vous etes...

My school was the next stop. The yellow stucco
building behind the field hockey field. I stood
up, my eyes straight ahead just like my father,
I looked out the big, wide, front windows and
walked toward the front of the bus.

My right hand gripped my canvas book bag
handle. My books between me and my father.

I walked past him as if he were someone I
didn't know. He didn't say anything, and I didn't
look back.

The doors opened. I wanted to turn and wave
goodbye to him, but I didn't. I stepped down and
heard the bus driver say "have a nice day."

In my head I said thanks, but no words came
out just a small polite smile. I looked down at my
shoes, both my hands on the canvas handle of my
book bag, the bus drove on, pushing air up my
front.

Air and dust and the bus and my father.

I stood at the crosswalk, the big yellow stucco school in front of me.

Je suis, the cars stopped.

Tu es, I started to cross.

Il est, the stink of car exhaust.

Vous etes. Dirt on yellow stucco.

Curb, sidewalk, the dark tunnel shortcut under the dining hall.

I couldn't remember the rest.

Panic hit my whole body.

I put my book bag down, and grabbed my small, spiral notebook.

My teacher said that notebook was the best for conjugating verbs and learning vocabulary because it had a line down the middle of each page. We'd write French on the left and the English to the right of that narrow maroon line on pistachio-green tinted paper.

Page after page of verbs, nouns. Language. My thumb and index finger pulling up the lower corners of each page.

My lips kept moving as if repeating the ones I remembered would help me remember the ones I forgot.

Je suis,

Tu es,

Il est,

Vous etes, past pages of vocabulary, I looked for my answer.

I'm gonna fail!

Je suis

tu es
il est
vous etes, chest and stomach clenched tight.
Then there it was:
Être | *To Be*
My eyes followed the line down the page to the
one I missed,
Nous Sommes.
And on the right side of that thin maroon line,
We Are.

SPAGHETTI & BULLIES

By sixth grade I had seen my parents host many elaborate cocktail and dinner parties. Mom would draft a menu and a to-do list specifying everything that needed to occur for a successful party, and she would spend days shopping and preparing the elaborate meals.

She would recruit me to polish the endless sterling silver and help set the table. "Of course you never want to confuse a salad fork with a dessert fork, dear."

Dad would select the wines to pair with the different courses and sometimes cases of champagne would be ordered.

From a young age, I would be introduced to the

guests early in the evening, usually during the cocktails. I would answer their questions about how I liked school, what my favorite subjects were, and where I wanted to go to college. Then it would conclude with the *nice to meet you*, and I would go off to my room. If I was lucky there would be delicious left-overs the next day, but that was rare.

Mother was an excellent cook. Instead of designing bridges and building what civil engineers build, she put her enthusiasm and attention to detail into hosting elaborate parties and well-designed evenings to please her guests and her husband. Their parties were popular not just for the food and drink but also as mom explained to me,

"To be a good hostess you want to make sure that your guests not only enjoy what they eat and drink but also the conversation. And that depends on who you invite. Your father and I like to bring people together from different cliques."

"What is a clique, mom?"

"Well, generally, it's when people who share similar interests keep company with each other to the exclusion of people with different views or interests. You know how you enjoy sailing with Kim?"

"Yes, of course, I love that!"

I idolized Kim, she was super-smart, graceful and she knew how to win races. Whenever she asked me to crew for her, I dropped everything else. Racing with her was a thrill. She knew how to push the boat and could read the wind and waves and strategize on the fly.

She'd yell through the wind to me,

"Hike out more and trim the jib, we're gonna catch those guys!"

My hands would grip that wet jib sheet as if my life depended on it. Soaking wet leaning out over the salty cold water of Narragansett bay. Wet Top Siders on my bare feet, my ankles hooked under the dirty canvas hiking strap, I would lean back as far as I could and hold. I got stronger, and her confidence in me made me feel more confident in what my body was capable of. She would always thank me when she accepted a win. One time she even gave me the silver plated cup we won, *so you will remember how much fun this was. Never be scared to push yourself and try new things.*

"Well," mom continued, "can you imagine her socializing with you and some of your other friends?"

I imagined it for a second thinking how cool it would be, but then the reality of it hit me: I don't think Kim would be interested in playing Batman and Robin, or Charlie's Angels, that's kid's stuff. So I said,

"Kim is much older, so that would be like Lydia playing superhero with us. It would be kinda weird."

"That's just my point, dear. You are similar to your father and me. You have many interests

with friends in different circles that don't neces-
sarily even know of each other."

I thought about the different people I liked
being around in addition to Kim:

Trish the RISD student who taught life drawing on Saturday mornings showed me how to
really "see" to draw.

*You have to look for a long time to see the lights
and shadows. Don't draw your idea of a face. Draw
what is actually there.*

Or Tammy from summer tennis clinic. We had
tea parties at the bottom of her pool and swam
like dolphins in the freezing waters off Beavertail
Point.

Or Susan who was in my grade, but I did not
know her until we both took Mrs. Patterson's
dancing class after school on Thursdays. We
bonded over our shared suffering of uncomfortable patent leather shoes, white gloves, and the
insufferable boys who stepped on our feet and
picked their noses. Soon she started sitting with
me at school lunch and we talked about Nancy
Drew Mysteries.

Then I thought of Miriam and Kathy and Anne
and Paige who were exclusive. They did not
really associate with other students.

"There are cliques in my class, too."

"I imagine there are."

"But we are all in the same class," I said.

"Well, even in a single grade, there will be girls
with different interests."

* * *

Paige used to be my best friend, but now she only associated with the popular girls who would become debutantes.

From first though fourth grades, Paige and I went to each other's house every other Friday.

Sometimes, she would come along as my family's guest for dinner at the University Club. We would get all dressed-up for a formal evening out. At the club, there was a cocktail jazz bar. We would sit at a candlelit table for four with the music of Thelonious Monk or The Glenn Miller Orchestra playing at low volume. Dad would order Shirley Temples for us while he and mom sipped their dry martinis. The four of us would listen to the music, and talk about anything and everything. It felt so grown-up and glamorous. Dad enjoyed talking about Big Band Swing and Jazz. After we finished our drinks, a man wearing a black tailcoat would show us to our table.

Paige was the first friend I had invited to join us for dinner at the University Club, and we would talk about it for days. Sometimes we would go to the school library to find the music we had heard, and play records in the listening booth. We would sing along and memorize our favorites: Paige liked to sing Chet Baker's *My Funny Valentine* and I loved Ella Fitzgerald's *Summertime*.

We liked discovering new foods too. Paige grossed out Susan one Monday during lunch describing the escargot we'd tried that weekend, "Snails smothered in melted butter. We *ate snails*, can you believe it? And they were good!"

Then one Friday, I overheard Paige's mother say to mine, *It's so odd, I found William Sr. and his mother listed in the Social Register, but I could not find you, the boys or Lydia. Can I rightly conclude that your youngest daughter will also not be a debutante?*

I heard my mother's short reply, that I would not be a debutante.

Then Paige stopped coming over.

I was devastated.

Then it got worse.

One Saturday, my parents and I were eating in the formal dining room at the club when I saw Paige and her parents walk in. She waved hello and her mother frowned at her. After they were seated at their table, Paige looked across the dining room at me and smiled. Her mother held up her linen dinner napkin instructing her to put it in her lap.

My mother leaned across the table as discreetly as she could to ask my father, "What are they doing here? They're not members, are they?"

"They are now. Bob asked me if I would recommend him for membership."

Mom sniffed her uppity sniff and said, "And

they won't even come over for a proper hello? Typical. New money, no manners."

Mom looked over at me, probably anticipating tears, but I was slowly learning to shut them off before they showed up.

The whole thing was confusing and painful enough but now hearing that my father helped them become members felt like a betrayal. *How could he do that?*

I was not good enough for Paige to be around since I was not going to be a debutante, and yet my father helped them become members of this exclusive club?

Insecurity creeped in with the possibility that my father put Bob's request ahead of my hurt at losing my best friend.

Perhaps he did not know what Paige's mother had said to mom. Perhaps he thought Paige and I were still friends, but it was pretty obvious something was wrong when she did not come over to our table to say hello.

He must not have known about what happened because if he did know, he certainly would put his daughter's well-being ahead of a favor for a man he barely knew. *Wouldn't he?*

Then the guilt followed, what an ungrateful daughter I was to think so poorly of my dad.

The sense of guilt and disbelief caused something else to grow like a Teflon shield over my heart. I had to ignore the hurt I felt, or accept the possibility that my father might have valued his relationship with an acquaintance more than his own daughter.

When Paige and I were assigned to get the milk and crackers for morning snack, she would talk and laugh just like when we were best friends, but then when she was around the popular girls, she would ignore me.

＊ ＊ ＊

I tried to picture Kathy and Miriam and Anne and Paige in the same room as me and Joy and Susan.

I had an idea:

"Mom, you said that people enjoy your parties, right?"

"Oh yes, very much."

"Even if they were not friends before?"

"Especially so, your father has been told more than once about new friendships that started at our dinner table."

Feelings of excitement at the idea of having a big successful party that everyone enjoyed, and hopes of being accepted by the popular girls or at least maybe Kathy and Miriam would stop making fun of the holes in my sweaters, and stop sneaking-up on me to stick their wet fingers in my ear when I sit in the front of the class. And maybe if the popular girls accepted me, then maybe Paige and I would be friends again.

"Mom?"

"Yes?"

"Could we, I mean, would you let me have a big party this year for my birthday?"

"How big?"

"I'd like to invite my whole class. You say new friendships are formed at your dinner table, maybe that could happen at my birthday this year."

"Well, parties take a lot of work, the bigger they are the more work to do."

"Please? I can help."

Her hesitation vanished. Then she said, "We could set up games in the ballroom and open presents in the living room. What would you like to eat?"

"Could we have spaghetti and that really good sauce you make?"

"Grandma's recipe? Well that will take some planning ahead, the sauce has to simmer for at least two days, but certainly. Why not. Spaghetti and meatballs it is!"

Mom grabbed a notepad from under the phone and started to make notes.

"Let's see, if we have twenty plus you that's twenty-one, so....maybe I will bake two or three birthday cakes just to make sure everyone can have seconds if they want to.

"And ice cream?"

"Yes, and ice cream. Balloons and other decorations too," she said, "It will be lovely."

Mom grabbed my hand. I could feel her excitement growing with mine.

"Let's talk it over with your father and see what he thinks. Now don't jump on him right when he walks in the door, let him unwind with his cocktail and newspaper. Then you can bring it up to him at dinner."

At dinner in between bites of broccoli and London Broil glazed with garlic butter I asked dad about my party.

"Inviting all your classmates for your birthday? I think that's a great idea," dad said.

"William, she has twenty classmates. That's quite a few mouths to feed. It will be very expensive."

"Isn't that about the number of people we had at our dinner party last month? You certainly made that a smashing success," dad said, "My boss is still talking about how delicious your chocolate torte was. He wants you to give your recipe to his wife."

They looked at each other in silence.

I looked back and forth like watching a tennis match waiting for a final answer.

Then mom looked at me and said, "Well, dear, your father approves so let's make this your best birthday party yet."

She took a sip of red wine and added,

"I don't think they will all show up, but you are welcome to invite them all."

The next day after school mom took me to Wayland Square to custom order invitations on fancy Crane Paper. Mom made sure they included an 'R.S.V.P.'

A week later we picked them up and brought them home. I sat at her desk in the sunroom behind the wall of tall succulent plants, and personalized each invitation trying to make my cursive writing as neat and pretty as possible. The following afternoon mom helped me lick all twenty envelopes.

At school I asked Ms. Edelhurst permission to hand them out, and when would be a good time to do so. Handing them out to each student, I explained it was for my birthday party and how nice it would be if they could make it.

Mom and I worked together on the menu and by the time my birthday arrived the following month, I was so focused on how to please everyone who would attend, that I almost forgot that the party was for my birthday.

I was so excited to show Anne and the popular girls my house and so hoped they would have a good time. They all RSVP'd *yes*, so they were all coming!

My deep roiling anxiety mixed with anticipation and my desire to host the best party ever was tempered only by mom keeping me busy with various tasks like stirring the meat sauce every hour for one whole Saturday, inflating the balloons, helping set the table, and folding twenty-one linen napkins into a fancy ring shape to stand on each place setting.

When everyone arrived, we played games in

the basement before lunch, and then Anne said, "Show us the rest of your house!"

"Yeah," Kathy said.

Mom said, "I will stay here with any girls who would like to continue the games or play ping pong."

About half the girls followed me upstairs to my bedroom. They wandered around looking at my books and things.

Kathy and Miriam walked over to my bed and touched my stuffed animals and Miriam said to Kathy, "She has no dolls."

The room fell silent, then Kathy said,

"Why don't you have any dolls? It's such a girly room all pink and white, but... no dolls?"

"That's kinda weird," Miriam said.

They both looked at me for an explanation.

"I dunno," I said, "Grammy gives me stuffed animals each Christmas and Easter and sometimes just because she wants to."

I loved my stuffed animals which were mostly all Steiff brand partly because they looked so real and mostly because Grammy gave them to me and I loved her very much.

I thought of my friend Brenda who I swam and sailed with in summer. She had Ken and Barbie dolls and we would play with them and dress them in different outfits, but I never asked for dolls of my own. I liked my stuffed animals.

Kathy picked-up one from my windowsill and laughed holding it up for everyone to see,

"Oh I remember this one - you brought it to school for show and tell."

A giggle went like a wave through my room, and all eyes were on Kathy holding my parakeet up in the air.

"Show and tell? Show what? It's a stuffed parakeet," Anne said.

I felt my face getting hot, and then even hotter at the awareness that it likely showed.

Kathy continued, "It was so funny. In third grade we had show and tell, and she brought it to school in a real cage with birdseed and newspaper and everything."

I remembered that day. I wanted to defend my actions, but the real story would only sound more pathetic, and bring the risk of tears.

What they didn't know, was that I had a real parakeet I planned to bring for show and tell, but he died two days before. I substituted my Steiff parakeet that Grammy had given me. It looked quite real, and I had told the class, "He's not real," but then pretended he was to show how to feed him, change his water, remove the tray and clean his cage. I got high marks from the teacher, but Kathy made fun of me for days, coming up to me at lunch and saying things like, "Does he sing to you? Does he poop? Do you imagine that too?" Then she and Miriam would walk away laughing.

My friend Joy saw my growing embarrassment, and interrupted the laughter with, "Let's see the rest of the house."

Walking down the hallway from my bedroom, Anne stopped when she noticed the two doors in the wall.

"What are these?" She asked.

I opened the smaller door, "This is a laundry chute."

"I have those at my house too," Miriam said to Anne, "I've shown you."

Anne nodded to Miriam and then said to me, "Can I look?"

"Sure," I said.

She put her head into the dark vertical tunnel that smelled of cedar wood, and looked down.

"I can't see anything. Does it go all the way to the basement?"

"Yes, if I had a flashlight you would likely see my dad's shirts at the bottom."

"Pretty cool huh?" Joy said.

Joy and I used to drop stuffed animals and notes down there like Little Will and I did when playing our spy games.

"And it's for laundry," Diane asked, "How does that work?"

As I was explaining to Diane, Anne pointed to the larger door next to the laundry chute and asked,

"And what's that one?"

"This," I said opening the door, "is a dumb waiter."

Her eyes got wide as she looked at the two dusty wooden shelves and dry darkened-with-age ropes.

"Do you use it?"

"Not really," I said.

Joy glanced over at me with a quick smile. I knew we were both thinking of the time we got caught using it to sneak Ritz crackers with cheddar cheese up to the second floor. The top shelf and ropes were so dusty-dry that there was dust on the cheese when it got to us; and the old metal pully system made enough noise going up the shaft that mom had heard it and caught us. But we did not share that with the group.

Instead I said, "I mean, it has been used, but it's not supposed to be."

"Could I get on it?" Anne asked.

"It's not for people," I explained. "It's an elevator for food and things."

Anne looked at Miriam and Kathy and said,

"I bet somebody really small could fit in there."

"Yeah," Kathy said, "Someone small and light, like Maggie. Maggie where are you?"

Maggie was quietly talking with Susan under the tall stained-glass windows on the landing between the first and second staircase.

"Maggie, come see this," Miriam called to her.

She slowly walked up the four stairs to the second landing with extra effort to go as fast as her braces would let her.

"It's not for people," I said again.

"Oh come on, this will be fun," Kathy said.

"Maggie, do you want to go for a ride?" Miriam

asked.

"What is it?" Maggie asked pushing her glasses up the bridge of her nose.

"It's a small elevator," Anne said, "c'mon get in, we can give you a ride downstairs so you don't have to walk."

Maggie moved closer; her shoulders rounded in more than usual.

Fear and anger started to well up in my gut.

* * *

I flashed on the face of my much older brother George, the sound of his laugh, the look on his face when he would ask me if I wanted to play *fifty-two card pick-up*.

It was always the same: his laugh as cards flew everywhere, followed by his command, *now get down on your hands and knees and pick them up. And count. Each one. Out loud.*

After I picked them up, he would insist he count them himself. *If any are missing you know mom and dad will be very upset. These are the ones they use to play bridge with the Jamisons.*

He would make me stand there and watch as he slowly counted each one, sometimes he would sneak one in his pocket or hold two together to torment me, *You missed one. Get down and look for it or we can start over if you want to.*

I realized the only way to stop his game was to hide the cards. So I took them and hid them in my sock drawer.

That night George decided to try something else. I forgot to put the cards back in Dad's desk drawer.

The following Saturday when the Jamison's came over for cocktails and bridge, mom came in without knocking and said,

"George told me you were playing with your father's cards. Where are they?"

I sheepishly took them out of my bureau behind my socks and handed them to mother.

"You know these are your father's cards and not for you to play with. Why did you take them when we told you not to?"

I told her about George and his game of fifty-two card pick up. She looked at me for a long time and then she said,

"Don't you ever lie to me young lady. Your brother would never do such a thing."

She grabbed my arm and took me across the hall to my bathroom and placed me next to the sink. Turned on the tap, and lathered the bar of Ivory Soap between her hands.

"We are going to wash your mouth out with soap young lady so you will learn not to lie," and she jammed her hand in my mouth.

The initial shock, gagging on the taste of the soap, her fingers hitting the back of my throat.

"Don't ever lie to me again. Never. Ever."

I stared at my blue Disney mug with Goofy on it and the tube of Ultra Brite toothpaste.

My mouth was no longer mine.

* * *

"It's not strong enough to hold a person," I said, "it's very old and the ropes are frayed."

Anne looked at me straight in the eye and held me in a stare that seemed an eternity. I thought of how Mom had told me to never get in there myself or allow anyone else to be in there. *It's made for casseroles not people. Don't ever crawl in there. You hear me? It will break, fall fifty feet to the basement and you will get hurt very badly.*

Mom was still in the down in the ballroom. I had asked her to let me show my guests around alone in hopes that I would impress them, but now I wished that she would magically appear at the top of the stairs. I often wished she would appear when George babysat me too, but I was on my own, and as usual, the house was too big for her to hear me even when I did call for help.

Finally with her eyes still on mine, Anne said, "Maggie, do you want to go for a ride?"

"Ok," Maggie said.

"We can't do that," I said, "my mother told me that people are never to get on this."

"Do you always do what your mummy tells you," Miriam asked.

Joy jumped in to help, "She's right, her mom told us it's forbidden."

"Ooooo, forbidden," Miriam said smiling at

Kathy.

The two of them grinning behind Anne. Maggie stood next to Anne now, looking smaller than ever. Anne looked over at Maggie, and then back at me. I had seen that face before.

Anne said with a curled lip,

"You are such a chicken. Most boring birthday party ever."

"Yeah you're being a big baby," Miriam said.

Kathy laughed and said loud enough for all the girls standing around to hear,

"Did you see all those stuffed animals she has on her bed?"

"And no dolls," Anne said, "what girl doesn't have any dolls?"

The three of them turned away, and started to walk down the stairs.

My heart racing, the palm of my right hand flat against the closed door of the dumb waiter. I looked at Maggie and said quietly, "I am so sorry."

She smiled a half-smile, turned and started to walk toward the stairs far behind the other girls.

I watched her walk away. Her green knee-socks between those metal rails.

I hated myself for what had just happened. I should have been mad at Anne, Miriam and Kathy, but I wasn't.

Instead, I turned it all on myself, imagining what mom would say if I told her:

What did you do to make them do that?

Or she might say,

Well young lady, that's what you get for wanting to show them the house yourself. You should have let me do it.

The dining room table was beautiful. Mom had tied colorful balloons to the chandelier and placed vases of fresh flowers at each end of the oak sideboard. She had accented the table with strategically placed bright Fiestaware bowls brimming with salted cashews and macadamia nuts. The sunlight was streaming in the dining room windows. It was perfect.

Anne, Miriam, Kathy and Paige sat next to each other to my left and Joy, Susan, Diane, and Maggie sat to my right. Mom added extra leaves to the oak table so it made a long oval with comfortable spacing for twenty guests and me. I sat in Dad's chair at the head of the table.

Mom served fancy Waldorf salads first and then the spaghetti and meatballs with fresh garlic bread. She brought each girl a plate and our cleaning lady, Patrice, stayed-on to help.

About half-way through our spaghetti course, Anne suggested we play the game of telephone, "It's where someone whispers something to a person and it goes around the table until the last person says it out loud and you see how much it changed or stayed the same."

"Ok," I said, "I can start."

"Usually," Miriam said, "it ends with the guest of honor, so you would go last."

I had never played it before, and was happy that the popular girls were engaging in my party. Just like mom said, people who didn't really know each other were connecting at my parent's table. Despite what had happened in the hallway upstairs, I was still hopeful for new friendships forming and for everyone to have a good time.

Anne looked at Joy sitting directly to my right and said, "Joy why don't you start?"

Joy thought for a second and then covering her mouth, she whispered something into Susan's ear.

And so it went, each girl hearing the phrase and passing it all around the table.

Finally, Kathy sitting next to me, leaned over and whispered in my ear,

"The spaghetti is hard."

"What? Say that again?"

She leaned in again, her voice with an edge to it, she said,

"The. Spa-geh-tee. Is. Hard."

I sat up taller trying to see if people had eaten their spaghetti. *How awful.*

Anne looked at me and said,

"Well, what was the phrase? You have to say it out loud, and then the person who started it tells what it was at the beginning."

I swallowed and said, "The spaghetti is hard?"

"What was it?" Miriam said, grinning.

I repeated myself, "The spaghetti is hard."

"Wait," Joy said, "that's not what I said."

"What did you say, Joy?" Kathy asked.

Joy was turning red, "I said, 'I forgot to bring a card'."

She looked at me, "Really, it's on the kitchen table at my mom's."

My face hot again and my words stuck in my throat, "That's ok, Joy."

"I am so sorry for anyone whose spaghetti wasn't cooked all the way. Does anyone want more spaghetti," I tried to make light of it, "hopefully softer this time?"

I noticed most of the plates were wiped clean including Anne's. A murmur went around the table, and I so wished I could control my blush; it always gave me away.

Anne, Miriam and Kathy were giggling among themselves. Paige was looking down at her lap, not laughing. I wondered why she was friends with them, but then again, I had wanted to be too.

Joy read my expression of *what now?*

"I will go tell your mother we are ready for the cake," she said, and headed into the pantry.

After the everyone left, mom sent Patrice home, and I helped in the kitchen, drying dishes and forks and spoons and glasses as she washed them all by hand.

"Well that was a success," she said.

"Not exactly," I said, and I told her what they said about the spaghetti being hard.

"Serving twenty-one plates of hot spaghetti is not easy," mom said, "to cook it all at the same time and have it just right."

I thought about dinners she had made for just as many people that seemed more complicated to me, but she had gone to a lot of trouble and I did not want to be ungrateful.

I didn't tell mom about the dumb waiter. I felt terrible about how they treated Maggie. I never should have let it get that far. I had wanted so desperately to impress Anne, Miriam and Kathy. Why had I wanted so much to impress them?

As for the spaghetti being undercooked, either they made it up, which would be mean. Or it was true. Either way, my birthday party did not go as I had hoped it would. I so wanted it to be a success like mom and dad's dinner parties.

The following Monday at school, Joy gave me my birthday card that she had forgotten to bring to the party. It was a huge card and very silly. She signed it *Your Friend Always, Robin.* I thanked her for being so helpful at the party. She smiled her broadest of smiles and said, "Anytime, Batman."

At gym before kickball started, I noticed Anne, Miriam and Kathy standing around Maggie, and Anne was swatting the pom-pom on Maggie's hat like a cat messing with a mouse.

Walking closer, I heard them taunt her, "Would you have gotten on that dumb waiter, huh? Or are you chicken too, four-eyes."

Not only did Maggie have to wear braces on both legs, but wore thick glasses, and they looked like they might grab for those too.

I found my voice,

"Hey!"

I stepped in between them and Maggie.

My body acted on instinct,

"If you want to hurt her, you have to go through me."

Our gym teacher was not there yet and when my brain caught up to my body, I remembered it was not smart to be confrontational, it could get bad very fast.

My heart was in my throat and I felt my chest and stomach tighten.

Kathy took one step closer to me and said,

"What are you going to do, send your attack parakeet after us?"

They all laughed hard.

"Leave Maggie alone," I said.

In that moment, my body knew I would defend her no matter what they tried.

"This is a waste of time," Anne said, "Let's leave the baby and four-eyes alone, you're perfect for each other."

The three of them walked over to Paige who had been watching us from a distance. She looked at me, then turned and walked away with them.

During kickball in gym that day, my unused adrenalin went into the ball and I kicked it hard towards mid-field. Anne caught it for a second with an audible "oomph", then dropped it, and I ran safely to third base. I could see Maggie on the sidelines, all glasses and smile.

After school that day, I started walking home when a blue Saab pulled over a few feet ahead of me, and the passenger window rolled down. I recognized it as the same car that dropped Maggie at school. Her mother leaned over towards the passenger window and invited me to come over that Friday.

"Yes, thank you, that sounds fun," I said.

"Our house is not as big as yours, but Maggie has lots of games to play. Would you like a lift? Your house is on the way, it's no trouble."

Once I was in the car, Maggie asked me, "Have you ever played Battleship?"

Thus began a new friendship. I became her bodyguard when she needed one and every other Friday afternoon I went to her house with a book and some Toll House cookies.

Maggie had more toys than I'd ever seen. We played chess, drew on her Etch-A-Sketch, took turns reading Hardy Boys and Nancy Drew books aloud, and she always won whenever we played chess or Battleship.

One day, she handed me her Lite-Brite and said,

"Show me what your parakeet looked like."

As I placed the yellow and green plastic pegs into the holes, they pierced the construction paper and filled with light. The shape of a bird with the greens and yellows of a parakeet began to appear, I started to tear up.

"It's silly, it was so long ago," I said, feeling embarrassed.

"That's ok," she said, "I understand, my dog got out of the yard, and was hit by a car when I was eight. I still miss him a ton."

"What was your dog's name," I asked.

"Max!"

"Was he big?"

Maggie smiled, "No, he was a tiny dog, fluffy and very small. My mom said the first time I saw him I pointed and said, "Max!" so that became his name. What was your parakeet's name?"

"Star," I said, "she loved to sit on my shoulder."

Maggie told me all about her adventures with Max and how much he enjoyed chasing frisbees and chewing her dad's shoes.

Later that afternoon, over mugs of hot cocoa, Maggie said,

"I wonder if they are friends up in heaven?"

We decided, somewhere up there wherever beloved pets go, a sensitive parakeet and a tough Pomeranian were the best of friends.

MIDOL &
TIGER BEAT

My sister Lydia scheduled her wedding for my thirteenth birthday.

"That way we will always remember the date," she said, "and my birthday present to you is that you will be my Maid of Honor."

She was engaged to a man named Eric, a Russian Studies graduate student she met during summer term. Lydia asked to wear our mother's wedding dress.

Mom had stored it carefully, tucked away, and when we opened the box we saw that it had aged beautifully. What was once pure white satin with a pearl inlay bodice and a modest train was now a beautiful, soft golden-ivory color.

I wondered if I too would be able to wear my mother's wedding dress someday, but was afraid to ask the question. Somehow I knew I would never wear that particular dress.

Lydia and my mother were in the master bedroom in front of the full-length mirror. She was telling mom the story again, and I never got tired of hearing it. Eric was into health and fitness, a runner, and one day when she was late leaving for class she saw him for the first time.

"I just knew," she said, "as he was jogging towards me, I had this feeling, this knowing-feeling in my whole body: *That's the man I will marry.* When I looked back, he was looking back at me."

"Please keep your arms up and hold still, Lydia," mom said.

My sister held her arms straight out not moving while mother placed pins along the seams around her upper torso and under the arms.

I sat cross-legged on the floor off to the side becoming the third point of a narrow triangle between them and the mirror.

My sister was talking excitedly about her future husband and all his plans after he finished graduate school, "His Russian is flawless and so many recruiters have been seeking him out. If he gets the job he wants with the State Department, he said we would live in Virginia."

She breathed shallow so as not to move the pins or get stuck by one near her armpit. She took three quick breaths and said, "And if we do live in

Virginia, I would be able to ride horses again!"

Lydia was a competitive equestrian. The blue ribbons still lined the walls above the picture moulding in her room. I liked to sit on her bed and count them. Thirty-six blue ribbons with gold lettering. She gave me one of her old riding jackets before she left for her year in France. It was too big for me, but I loved to wear it when Little Will and I were on our covert missions in East Berlin.

"How cool would it be if Eric became a real spy," I said. Lydia smiled.

My industrious mother was focused on the task at hand. My grandmother was a wonderful dressmaker out of necessity, and she taught my mom and my aunt excellent dressmaking and sewing skills in the years before the war. Mom was so frugal that she would darn my father's socks when they got a hole rather than buying a new pair.

I started to feel cramps in my stomach. I thought I might be getting sick or just my anxious tummy. I went into my mother's bathroom and when I pulled down my underwear, a wave of panic went through me at seeing two dark spots in the cotton crotch.

"I'm bleeding!"

I heard my sister laughing.

Mom without missing a beat calmly said,

"You started your period. You'll find a belt and napkins in the cabinet next to the sink."

I knew what a period was, but I wasn't ready to start it now, less than a week before my sister's wedding?

With my underwear around my knees, I waddled over to the cupboard, and pulled out the pad and belt. I assembled this hideous contraption consisting of a thick long pad that I pulled the front and back ends through what looked like an ugly bigger version of my mother's garter belts.

The pad was thick and bulky and the elastic belt around my waist rough against my skin. I wiped off the small bit of blood, and pulled up my underwear positioning everything best I could. I smoothed my school uniform skirt down over my underwear and thighs. The pad was too long and the ends of it formed visible bumps in the front and back of my skirt.

It was horrifying to think of going to school with that. Everyone would be sure to notice it. I feared I would be teased mercilessly.

I had wanted for so long to grow up to be like my sister and Hope, and now I wondered, was this what it meant to be a woman?

I washed my hands and walked back to where I had been sitting. Ugh. It felt like I had a towel bunched up between my legs when I walked. I sat down carefully as to not move anything out of place.

"You, got, your peer-eee-ood," my sister teased in her taunting sing-songy voice.

"Lydia, that's enough," mom said, and she

looked over at me for a second, "find everything alright?"

"Ouch!" Lydia said.

"Well don't move. And stop teasing your sister," mom said.

Mom with a pin between her lips said, "We'll get you some sanitary pads and your own belt tomorrow."

I went into my dad's den to call my best friend from school to share the news. Joy was what mom called an *early bloomer*. She was already wearing bras and had started her period the year before.

"That's great," she said cheerfully, "but you really should get tampons. They are less messy and much more comfortable once you get used to them."

I got lightheaded and had a sudden wave of pain along with the sensation that my insides were going to drop to the floor.

"I gotta go," I said and hung up.

I walked slow down the stairs and laid down on the couch hoping for the pain to pass.

My father folded his newspaper and pulled off his reading glasses.

"What's the matter? Are you not feeling well?"

"Woman stuff, Dad. I got my...it hurts real bad."

I could feel the tears coming up.

Why am I such a baby?

"Where's your mother?"

"She's upstairs with Lydia, taking-in the dress a bit."

Dad sat his paper down, came over to me and pulled the throw blanket down from the back of the couch. He covered me and pulled it up to just under my chin and then smoothed my hair back off my face.

"Try to rest. I will be back in a little bit."

About a half hour later, dad was standing next to me with a brown paper bag in one hand and a glass of ginger ale in the other.

He set the glass down on the coffee table coaster and handed me the paper bag.

"Here, this might help you feel better," he said.

Inside there was a bottle of Midol and the latest copy of Tiger Beat magazine with Sean Cassidy and Leif Garrett on the cover. My surprize at what he had done for me came out in a squeak, "Thank you, daddy!"

He walked back to his chair and continued reading his newspaper.

The two Midol went down almost too easy with the ginger ale. I laid back down under the blanket waiting for the knifing pains to subside. If this was how much it hurt to have a period, how much more painful would it be to have a baby? The thought of that scared me.

I opened the magazine to distract myself from the sharp pains and then the cramps stopped just as abruptly as they had started. The Midol worked like magic!

With the pain gone, my whole body started to relax. I felt so safe there on the couch with my dad a few feet away reading in his chair.

He had brought me comfort and showed me a nurturing side of himself that I had not seen before.

When I was little he taught me important things like how to tie my shoes, how to swim, and ride a bike. In the last few years it had been more about grades and how I was doing in school.

I thought of the way Hope had described my father to me years before, *he was kind and supportive...Your father was wonderful to us.*

My mom upstairs with Lydia preparing her dress for the big day most girls dream about, and I was content being near my dad who saw me without judgment, and helped the pain go away.

PART 2:
TEENAGE
IMPRINTS

*Summer 1979 -
Christmas 1981*

FOUND & LOST

The summer I turned 14 was the first year I had a job away from home. I was going to be a live-in nanny, helping my brother William and his wife Hope care for their sons Little Will and Benji.

I had held odd jobs cutting grass, babysitting and pulling weeds in my grandfather's huge garden the summers before that, but this was a fancy job, a real job, with weekly pay and everything. Hope, had talked with my mom about it, and when I asked if I could go, mom had sniffed her uppity sniff and said,

"That's fine. But she is paying you way too much money." I was thrilled she agreed to let me go. I felt so grown up, I could almost forget my mother's disapproving tone. Almost.

The movie *Jaws* was one of the big summer

blockbusters a few summers before and Hope had given me the paperback book to read. She loved to talk about sharks - especially when we were swimming.

One Saturday during that amazing month of July we were all at the beach and my brother offered to watch the boys while Hope and I went out for a swim alone.

Hope was a strong swimmer, and after we got several feet away from shore, we were treading water in ten feet of clear Cape Cod blue, when she asked, "Should we swim out to the raft today?"

It was high tide, and the raft was at least another twenty yards out in what seemed much deeper water. There were several people on it, dancing around, jumping off the diving board, pulling up on the ladder and leaping out for another turn.

"No this is fine," I said.

Salt water dripped from her short, light brown, wiry hair onto her thick tan shoulders. Her eyes a deep heather blue. I wanted to be a grown-up like her, beautiful like her.

She started laughing at me, "You're scared."

"No. No, I'm not."

My heart was racing. I tried to hide it.

I was treading water and watching the people on the raft. Maybe I should swim out there, but I don't know them.

One tall, blond boy wearing light blue swim trunks looked so happy. "Cannonball!" he shouted out then launched himself off the diving board two feet up and out, knees to chest making a huge splash. People on the raft whooped and hollered.

Sharks are attracted to loud noise and movement.

"Duh-nuh, duh-nuh." Hope grabbed my left thigh. I screamed. I turned around, and there she was - laughing her round full laugh that was pure joy.

A small bit of pee escaped from my green one piece Speedo bathing suit.

"That's not funny." I said coughing up salt water.

I swam a few feet away and dove down below, reaching though the clear water for the sandy bottom. I always felt more comfortable and fearless underwater because I could see what was below. My body moved easily though the water. I imagined I was a dolphin or a mermaid. I was lithe, longer and more flexible than last summer.

✽ ✽ ✽

My father taught me how to swim at the age of four in the dark, cold waters of Narragansett Bay. He would stand on the steps on one side of the dock up to his waist in the water at high tide. I would stand on the parallel set of steps on the other side of the dock.

Even though it was a bright sunny day, the water underneath the dock between those two stairs was in shadow, so I could not see into the water. He was less than ten feet away, but the space of black water underneath the dock between me and him seemed a gulf too far.

His arms reaching out he said, "Just come to me. I'll catch you."

Finally, I splashed over to him wildly in the brisk cold water attempting my first dog paddle.

"That's it!" His big smile and open arms made me feel triumphant.

By seven years old I was a strong swimmer, but still fearful of swimming in deep dark water. It wasn't until I started snorkeling and could see beneath the surface that the underwater world became my comfort zone.

* * *

Now swimming with Hope at the Cape, I was eyes-open underwater with no sharks in sight. Treading water Hope's thick legs moved slowly. The green and white flowered pattern of her bathing suit shimmered underwater. She wore the same style as my mom complete with a modest skirt.

Coming up for air, the weight of my water-soaked hair tugged at my scalp.

Water-bubble sounds of Hope humming the *Jaws* theme and her laughter chased me all the way back into shore.

The sand was so dry it squeaked with every

step. My brother and the boys had a huge sandcastle under construction. Little Will carried buckets of sea water to fill the large moat while his younger brother, Benji, shaped the wet sand into towers using his mold and shovel so carefully.

"And what's the part of the castle where the arrows are shot from?" my brother asked his sons.

"The turret!"

"Turret, that's right Benji. Good job!"

I stepped to the other side of the chairs and snuggled down into the warmth of my towel on the hot sand. The salt water evaporated quickly tightening my skin and tickling my ears.

Sun warmed the back of my legs, shoulders and side of my face. Hope sat in her low beach chair. Slow falling droplets of seawater darkened the dry sand below her chair.

"Anyone ready for lunch?" Hope asked.

"Yes, thank you" we almost all said in unison. Eyes closed. The hollow sound of her lifting off the Igloo cooler lid.

"OK, come on over," Hope said.

I could feel the energy of Little Will and Benji running over. The rumble of ice. The crinkly sound of waxed paper wrapped sandwiches.

"We have Tuna, ham or PB and J."

"Peanut butter, please," Little Will said.

"For me too mommy," Benji always copied his older brother whom he adored.

"Ham sounds good to me," my brother said.

My stomach growled. I dug my toes deeper into the hot sand. Eyes closed, I did not want to move, the happiness and sense of belonging on that perfect day was magical. I wanted to soak it all in to imprint it into my whole body and keep it forever.

I felt Benji's small sandy foot on the back of my calf. "Aunt Beth, are you going to have a sandwich?"

Mom never allowed us to eat lying down.

Sit up and eat like a lady.

I turned over and sat up, "Yes, I would love a tuna sandwich, please."

"Here you go." Hope said.

Benji jumped in between us, "I do it."

Benji carefully took the waxed paper wrapped sandwich from Hope's tanned hand, and carried it over to me in both hands as if he were presenting me with a gift.

"Thank you Benjamin, that is very kind of you!" I said.

Hope handed him his peanut butter and jelly sandwich, and he skipped back over to his father and sat down next to him.

I watched as Hope took more things from the cooler. Her fingers were long and tanned. I wished for elegant hands like that instead of the square-fingered ones I got from my Dad. Her gold wedding band sparkled with a single drop of saltwater that caught the sunlight.

Hope taught me how to make sandwiches that summer: rich, thick tuna fish sandwiches with tomato and thin slices of celery on Pepperidge Farm bread and just the right amount of mayo.

Mom didn't approve of what Hope prepared for meals. Ever since Benji told her last summer about how much he liked marshmallow and peanut butter sandwiches and declared that peas came from a can, not from grandpa's garden, well mom was horrified.

I was still hungry and wanted to have a second sandwich, but could hear mom's voice in my mind, *why anyone would prefer store bought bread to homemade is beyond me.*

I asked for a diet Tab soda instead.

Two hours later after sandcastle empires were built and destroyed, and treasures were found from walking the beach and snorkeling in the waves, it was time to head home.

"Shotgun!" I called out. I broke into a sprint, ran up behind Little Will, and tapped him on his shoulder as I passed him. His legs reached in their wet nylon-swim shorts behind me. My hand reached the door first.

"Not fair! You have longer legs!" Little Will tumbled into the car with his towel, bucket, mask, snorkel and nylon mesh diver's bag.

Just like our imaginary games we made up at Christmas time, pretending to be dinosaurs or spies, in the summer we hunted for treasure and sharks!

That day Little Will's dive bag carried his treasures of green sea glass and sand dollars. It was a good day.

As we pulled up the house, Hope's brother Larry was hosing down a row of bluefish he caught that day.

"Go ahead and get showered right away," Hope said.

My brother was already out of the car and walked directly to the cooler and took out a beer, deftly popping the can open and taking his first long draw with one hand.

Larry turned the hose on me Little Will and Benji, making us sprint from the hot car to the outdoor shower. After rinsing the sand off us under cold-cold water, we headed inside.

Still in my bathing suit and with my towel snug around my waist, I went into the kitchen. Ocean swimming, sun and snorkeling always made me hungry.

I rinsed off a peach from the fruit bowl on the counter and started to devour it. The sweetness could not fill my mouth fast enough.

Peach juice dripped down my chin and into the brushed steel sink.

I could see my brother and Larry through the kitchen sink window reviewing the catch of the day. A line of bluefish laid out on the grass. I counted eight - each one must have been two or three feet long like small sharks all silvery blue-gray, reflecting the sun.

The men were preparing to gut the fish and fillet them. Two would be for dinner, and then they would ceremoniously prep the rest for the freezer. I opened the window, and their voices came in on the warm breeze.

"Are you heading out again tomorrow?"

"Sure," Larry said, "when they're running like this, you gotta get as much as you can, while you can."

"Good, I will join you. Maybe I can do some spear fishing off the boat too," my brother said.

I wiped the juice off my chin and reached for another peach. The peach fuzz smoothed under the water pressure from the tap. Drying salt water started to tickle inside my ears. My skin felt tight. I was getting darker each day. I wanted to be a beautiful dark golden brown like Hope.

In the summers when I was outside all the time, dad would call me his "little brown berry." I loved it when he called me that. I missed dad, but not so much mom.

I could hear her critical voice as if she were standing right there in the kitchen with me:

"Don't eat standing up, it's bad for your digestion."

"Don't eat between meals, you'll ruin your appetite."

"You're having another one??"

I knew how her eyes would settle on my waist while she talked. My stomach muscles tightened standing over the sink feeling the sting of her words even though she was miles away.

Mom would always tell me I had colt legs when I was younger, but once I turned thirteen, she was certain I was getting fat. I wasn't, but I started to feel fat from the inside.

Larry held up a bluefish by its gills and inserted the buck knife right below the head, and sliced down the white belly to its tail.

He lifted one side grabbed the insides swept them out into the bucket.

Little Will called to me from upstairs, "Ok. I'm done!"

I looked at the remaining part of the delicious peach in my hand. I squeezed it hard until I felt the sharp tip of the pit poke into my palm. Juice and peach pulp oozed between my fingers and down the inside of my wrist. I threw it away and rinsed my hands.

Heading upstairs, I slowed to look closer at the numerous family pictures in the foyer and all along the wall up the stairs. I was not used to seeing so many pictures around. It was very different from how my parents decorated, and I liked it.

There was only one photograph hung on the many walls of my parent's house. It was a large, gold-framed candid shot of William Jr., Lydia and George, all dressed-up and laughing. The image of it was burned in my mind and I recalled it going up the stairs. William Jr. had his mouth open at the beginning of a smile, as if he had just told a joke or heard one and was starting to laugh. George was in profile smiling looking over at William Jr., and Lydia was in the middle looking at the camera with a smile that showed she thought it funny too. It was taken outside in front of a large fancy tent. It may have been William Jr. and Hope's wedding.

That photo of my much older siblings was centered above the living room couch, prominently placed for all guests to see. They all looked happy, beautiful and perfectly photogenic like models or French film stars.

In that moment walking up the stairs of the Cape Cod house that afternoon, looking at the black and white framed photos of Hope's extended family and ancestors next to new color photos of her and William Jr. and the boys, the contrast hit me. Hope's entire family history was displayed, but my parents had only the one photo of my siblings framed and hung in the living room. In our huge, cold, cavernous house, that was the only photo. There were no images of me.

Invisible.

"Can we play badminton before dinner?" Little Will asked me from the top of the stairs.

"Let's see if we have time, buddy," I said.

"Me too, me too," Benji shouted. The door to the boy's room was open and Hope was pulling a shirt over Benji's head.

"Can I help you with dinner prep?" I asked her.

"Sure, how about a big salad? And there's time

to play a little badminton with the boys after you take your shower," Hope said.

"Yay! Yay!" Benji jumped up and down. "Bat-mitten!" He was such a happy boy always singing and dancing.

"Hold still," Hope said, let's get your shorts on right young man, one leg at a time."

After my shower, I didn't want to get dressed. Nothing felt right. Even the soft, plush towel was too much. I started to pat myself dry, then gave up, and decided to let the water evaporate off me.

My skin was so sensitive, not burned, but spilling over with the warm sunlight of that perfect day. Fine hairs stood up straight on my arms. Anything other than air was too much. With my back and shoulders still wet, I put on my bra. The straps felt uncomfortable, but I was now showing too much to go without one.

My body was changing every day. Some days I longed for the time when I didn't have to wear a bra at all, and sometimes I loved that I was finally getting breasts like my sister.

I pulled on my track shorts with my favorite powder blue Lacoste shirt. Raising up my shoulders, the shirt stuck to my damp skin.

I pulled my long damp un-brushed hair back from my face with two barrettes, and headed downstairs toward the smell of fresh cut grass, and the sound of my brother's voice.

The front door was open and everyone was out on the lawn.

"Stand back, boys. Daddys got a knife."

William Jr. slit open a bluefish from gills to tail with one swift motion. More pink guts slooshed out into the tan plastic bucket.

Little Will ran over to me swinging his badminton racquet.

"Is that your sword, Prince Caspian?"

"Yes!" he said.

And Benji was right behind him swinging a badminton racquet that was almost as tall as he was.

I walked to the far side of the lawn. The badminton net was always up that summer. It divided the front lawn into two large areas of soft grassy green.

The whistling birdie only had time to go back and forth over the net for a few hits when Hope called out to me from the front door,

"Your Mom's on the phone."

"I'll be right back," I yelled over the net to my nephews, set my badminton racquet down, and headed back toward the house. The grass was so soft and warm under my bare feet.

Going from the hot sun into the hallway my skin puckered with goose bumps. The black and white tiles of the front hall were cool. I picked up the receiver from the front hall table.

"Hi Mom!" I said a little out of breath and smiling.

"Hello," she said, "are you having a good time with your brother?"

"Yes, and today we - "

She cut me off with "Your father and I bought a house this weekend," she said.

"We setup the badminton set...wait, what?"

"In New Hampshire."

"New Hampshire?"

I only knew it from the two times we had gone up there for vacation.

"We leave in two days."

I was trying to follow her words.

My brain scrambled.

"We are moving," she said, "to New Hampshire."

Her tone sounded irritated now, like I wasn't getting it.

My feet went ice cold.

My eyes jumped from the photos of smiling people on the wall to the railing along the stairs to the black and white tile to my feet.

I couldn't feel my feet.

"But I have another month here with Hope and the kids."

Mom talked over me, as if I had said nothing,

"Hope has agreed to release you from your so-called baby-sitting job there a month early."

"What?"

My hands got cold.

In that moment, someone else was holding the phone.

It wasn't my hand anymore.

"*Moving*?" My brain screamed.

It was like that recurring nightmare I had in first grade where I would scream in the downstairs front hall bathroom, but no sound would come out.

"You will be going to the public school."

"Can't I stay where I am?"

I loved my school that I had attended forever. Although I was only in 8th grade, I had classes in Latin, French, Music, American Literature, History, Creative Writing, Gymnastics and Painting. And my best friends in the world: Joy, Susan and Maggie.

"What about my friends, and school, and gymnastics?" I asked.

"It's all set."

Then as if talking about the weather, her tone went from irritable-serious to cheery-light, and she switched subjects as she would for the many painful years ahead.

"I understand your brother caught bluefish today!"

I squeezed my eyes tight until I saw spots behind my eyelids.

"Well no, actually, it was Larry, Hope's brother who caught fish today. I am going to cook them up in butter just like I did with the baby blues I caught last summer off the pier, remember?"

She sniffed and then, "Well, you enjoy that dear. You know, I never really liked bluefish, only swordfish for me. And that Larry...he drinks too much."

My face got hot. My eyes moved from the generations of Hope's family photos along the staircase to the stairs to the floor, the banister, trying to focus. Trying to force my brain to catch up.

I had the sensation I had stepped out of time.

My throat was closing-up on me, in a whisper I asked,

"Why can't I stay here? Why do I need to leave now?"

Maybe she did not hear me, maybe I did not even say it out loud, but what she said was, "OK dear, we will see you tomorrow. Bye, bye."

The hallway had grown darker in the last couple minutes. The sun had moved. I walked outside and stood on the front steps for a minute. Stiffening my body and taking a deep breath I tried my best to be a big girl, just get on with things like mom and dad had always taught me.

Benji ran up to me smiling he held out my badminton racquet to me.

Everything blurred.

My body heaved.

Then arms around me - catching me - Hope's arms. The same arms that showed me how to make snow angels.

Hope softly said to little Benji and Little Will looking on, "It's ok, she's just sad. How about you boys head over and see if you can go help Uncle Larry with those fish."

I was so embarrassed. I didn't want to cry.

What a baby I was. I could hear my brother's heavy walk approaching in the grass, "What the hell happened?"

I was embarrassed to be crying in front of my brother.

I could feel the movement of Hope's arm waving him away.

Then to me, "Let's go sit over here for a minute."

She wrapped her arm around my shoulder and led me to the small side garden filled with roses. A red and pink blur through my tears. We sat on the cement garden bench. Gargoyles perched on either side of us.

"Ok," Hope said, "tell me what happened."

My brain had just stalled out. I didn't understand what was happening. It was all so sudden. "We're... moving...I guess?"

She stared back towards the house, scratching her left knee.

"I know," she said. "Your Mom asked me if you could leave early before the summer's out. She asked me if I could get a replacement to help with the kids."

"But I want to stay."

I had stopped crying now. I wanted her to look at me, and yet I didn't. I was embarrassed by my puffy eyes, my nose and face all red and gross.

Maybe this was just a bad dream, and I would wake up to find myself under thick quilts in my room at the end of the hallway.

Everyone said the fresh bluefish and salad that we ate at dinner were delicious.

I could not taste a thing.

After the boys were tucked-in and read to, Hope and I went to my room to brush my hair as she'd promised.

Both sitting on my bed, I studied the room to memorize it, knowing that was the last night I would see it. I loved that room. Exposed wood walls. The nightstand a pale green with 19th century wood showing through on the worn spots. The knotty, woven rug on the floor – of blues, greens and purples like the sea glass colors Little Will and I cherished.

The dormer window was open. Crickets pulsed their evening song in a poetic rhythm.

I had fallen into the rhythm of the meaning of "family" that I had not known until that summer and I did not want to leave. It felt so safe. So full of laughter and joy and the newness of belonging.

Hope had been so kind to give me the job. She was paying me real money per week to look after my nephews and play games and have fun. It was a huge gift, and I would do whatever she asked me to, and joyfully.

If she wanted me to help her make sandwiches for the kids, she would show me how they liked them, and then I would be the sandwich maker whenever she asked.

Load the dishwasher, ok.

Read certain books to the boys while she ran errands, no problem.

I learned the foods they liked and would prepare lunch and sometimes all meals for the boys while she and my brother took time for themselves all afternoon and into the evening.

I learned so much from her and it was never through shame or criticism but rather by her example and encouragement, and sometimes gentle correction, with an occasional well-deserved ribbing, like when I tossed Benji's cobalt blue socks in with a load of white bedsheets. But she was never harsh or razor-critical like my mother often was.

At the same time Hope was building my self-confidence and showing me how to take on increasing responsibility, she also was a mother to me.

Like brushing or braiding my hair. I could not recall the last time my mother showed me that kind of nurturing affection and care.

"Did you like that new de-tangler?"

"Yes," I said, "it smells like strawberries." "Yes, and it made your hair shiny and soft." She kept the bristles moving through my long hair. It felt so good. Simple warm comfort of a mother and daughter.

I picked at a stray thread on the quilt and I remembered how different it was with my Mom. There would be no more Hope brushing my hair that summer. No more warmth.

"Do you remember the first time you brushed my hair?" I asked.

Hope laughed. "Yes," she said, "it took a long time...you were quite a feral child with that tangle of hair."

Back then, years ago when I was just five, that was the first time. She had to cut out a snarl at the base of my skull behind my right ear the size of a quarter. She did it skillfully so you couldn't tell what was missing unless you lifted up my hair and looked for the gap. I never told anyone.

"Well, I was just a kid then," I said.

"Yes" she said.

Her hands were long and delicate yet strong. An imprint. A positive, nurturing one.

"You were much younger then."

She tugged the brush a little and leaned-in, "now that you are a young lady you can remember to brush your hair like this *every* night like this? One hundred strokes, OK?"

"OK," I said.

I started to tear up again. I hated being such a baby.

She placed her other hand on my back, directly behind my heart and said,

"You are a strong, beautiful and intelligent young woman. Promise me you will remember that. You can always call or write. We will come visit."

Her hand dropped away and she continued brushing my hair. I never saw Hope cry, ever, but her voice sounded full of tears when she said, "You know your brother and I... love you very much...always will."

"I know," I said.

But I didn't know.

In that moment all I knew was that the happiness I felt all those days at the Cape would now be behind me.

It reminded me of when Little Will and I would play during the holidays and mom would accuse us of being tired. *Nap time, you two!*

I was about to leave my best friends, my school my home, everything that I had always known and for the first time in my life I felt respected, seen, and valued for something other than my grades on my report card or how well-mannered I behaved when mom and dad showed me off at their cocktail and dinner parties.

This was a new lesson one of being given the serious real responsibility of taking care of others, and also I was deeply cared for, respected and nurtured by Hope.

That was all a very positive imprint, but that day, during just those few minutes on the phone with my mom, the older, competing imprint got bigger, deeper and became one that I would live out over and over again for years trying to fix.

The message seeped into my subconscious that I did not deserve to have that kind of happiness. I did not belong in such love.

That kind of safety and heart-bursting joy of

that idyllic July was for someone else and if by mistake I had it, the moment was fleeting or worse I would be punished for being so ebulliently happy.

I had found family, found a sense of belonging and love. Now, it would be taken away.

So too it seemed almost worse to know the feeling and then have it taken away than to never know it at all.

My eyes stung from crying so much. I couldn't hear the crickets anymore, just the sound of blood rushing in my ears. She pulled me into to the softness of her bright yellow sundress.

Her tan arms enveloped me and she rocked me gently like a baby.

I didn't want to leave this. Leave them.

Leave our afternoon naps when we all snoozed in the sunlight or laughed in tickle-fest dog piles.

The loud, family game nights of Clue, Life or Yahtzee when Benji would dance around the room with my brother's baseball cap, chanting "Yahtzee, Yaht-zee! Yaaah-tz-zeeee!" in between turns no matter which game we were playing.

Or when my brother showed me how to buddy breathe for the first time in deep water using his scuba tank.

Or when Benji would embellish the story of Robin Hood insisting that Maid Marian and Princess Leia of Star Wars were actually sisters. And that only *his* closet was the real one that went to Narnia.

Or how Little Will liked it best when I made his egg salad sandwiches with a layer of sliced pickles.

"I don't want to move," I said.

I turned and looked back at Hope. She put the brush down, and hugged me again letting me cry until I stopped.

It felt so safe, so right, so foreign.

She put a new box of tissues by the bed and tucked me in. Kissed me goodnight on my forehead like she did when I was younger and turned out the light.

The next morning, I woke to the soft sunlight and faint sound of a mourning dove's coo outside my window.

Safe and peaceful.

And then, the slow waking recall seeped into my consciousness of the day before. I pulled Hope's grandmother's patchwork quilt up over my head.

Downstairs, my brother, Hope, and the kids were eating breakfast.

"I made waffles," Hope said.

I sat down at the table in silence. I put on a smile. I did not want to cry again.

My brother was asking the questions I had wanted to ask but didn't.

I finally jumped in and spoke,

"What about my bedroom? I have to pack the stuff in my bedroom don't I?"

"No," Hope repeated what she said to my

brother, "your mom said that the movers already packed the *whole* house. All of it. They are loading the truck today."

The thought of a strange man rifling through my underwear drawer went through my head,

"My clothes. My books?"

"Yes," she said, "All packed."

My brother, William, looked at me.

"Damn," he said as he pushed his chair away from the table and walked back into kitchen.

"Any more waffles?"

"In the oven," Hope said.

My brother came back out, kissed Little Will and Benji on their heads, and sat down a plate heaped high with warm golden brown perfect waffles.

I could barely look up at these faces of a happy family. A lump of tears in my throat, but I did not want to cry again. Not in front of the boys. I had to be strong. I wanted to remember this summer always.

Benji insisted he could cut his waffles without his parent's help using a smaller size butter knife.

Little Will ate in silence for several bites, taking it all in, and then looked across the table at me and said,

"Well...if there are lakes near grandpa and grandma's we could still go snorkeling and fishing next summer."

"That's a great idea, buddy," I smiled "I am

going to miss you guys so much."

I looked over at Hope hoping to hear her say, "Your mom and I talked again last night, and you are staying here until September as planned."

But she didn't say that.

Instead, she held out the serving plate and said, "Waffle?"

HIGHWAY TO HELL

September. New state, new school, new life. No friends. In a dark parking lot surrounded by ancient pine trees, dad waits with me in the pitch-black hour before dawn.

"Do you have everything?"

"Dad, it's the first day, I don't know what I need."

Dad and I sit in his new Jeep Grand Wagoneer that he purchased the day after we arrived in New Hampshire.

"We need to be able to get around in the snow," he said to justify the large expense to my frugal mother.

In silence, we sat on soft leather seats, surrounded by warm wood paneling.

Alone together at the bus stop.

"Your mother and I were talking about spending Christmas in Michigan again this year with Lydia and Eric, what do you think about that? We had a good time last year, didn't we?"

"Yeah," I said, "that would be nice."

The town we moved to has one general store with a gas pump.

No fire station.

No library.

No school.

In a town that still has more wildlife than people, you don't need much. Not every house even has electricity or running water.

We lived in a community inside this town. A new community for retirees, but it was just as isolated and rural as the town.

And this is where my father chose to move us to. Running away from whatever it was he was running away from.

Dad opened a small door in the dash, and pulled out a black plastic square with a coil attached.

"This is a CB radio, so we can call for help if we ever need to."

He turned it on long enough to hear a burst of static, when a yellow school bus pulls into the parking lot.

The bus turned around behind us and parks parallel to us.

"Have a good day," dad says, "I will meet you right here after school."

I get out of the car wearing my 'weekend' clothes. The only clothes I own other than my school uniform.

Mondays through Fridays for the last ten years of my life, I attended private school and had worn a uniform.

Now that I will be attending public school, mom said I would have to make do with my weekend outfits.

I was not used to thinking about clothes. For ten years my only clothing decision during the week was what color socks to wear: green, gray or blue.

Mom said jeans were not proper for school, so although September is still warm, she made me wear my tan corduroys with one of my white Lacoste polo shirts that I used to wear with my uniform. I chose my favorite weekend Fair Isle sweater.

Dad drives away and I board the yellow school bus. The bus driver wears a weathered face. He does not smile or talk. Since mine is the first stop, the bus is empty. I choose to sit close to the front.

After I sit down, the bus driver looks at me in his wide rear-view mirror and says,

"We're just waitin' on one more here."

My eyes linger in his for a second. I smile and look down. The green vinyl seats are sunken and cracked. The seat across from me has gray duct tape along the front edge and sides.

Another car pulls into the parking lot, circles around the bus and stops parallel. A boy with shoulder-length, dark curly hair gets out of a silver Oldsmobile sedan.

With his long face, spotty complexion and rounded shoulders, he looks even more miserable there than I am. He ambles up the steps and walks all the way to the back of the bus. I stare at the bright red tail-lights of the Oldsmobile as it drives away in the bluish-purple dawn.

The bus driver starts the engine and closes the door. He checks his side mirrors, and we exit the parking lot.

School does not start until after 8:00, but the bus ride takes over ninety minutes to pick up the kids from surrounding towns. The towns are so rural, I will attend a high school several miles away in a different county. Everything I had known for 14 years changed during that one phone call from mom that day at the Cape. *Your father and I bought a house this weekend...in New Hampshire. We leave in two days.*

I look out the window at the passing scenery like I'm watching a film of someone else's life.

Where am I?

I am out of place and time.

The bus ride is so rough I involuntarily bite the inside of my cheek and tongue more than once. I taste iron in my mouth.

I learned to clench my jaw on those morning

bus rides. Bracing one more part of my body for impact.

6:30 AM.

The bus slows to a stop where a large overweight man wearing a white undershirt and jeans stands by a mailbox.

Behind him is a house tucked back from the road. I look closer at the house, and notice the walls are black with printing on them, and realize the house has no siding.

I have never seen a house without its outsides. I thought maybe it was new construction until I notice the tattered roof shingles and a small trail of smoke coming from the chimney.

The man yells back over his right shoulder towards the house and takes a long draw from a can he's holding.

I know that red and white pattern: it's the same beer my brother William Jr. drinks since forever.

❖ ❖ ❖

Beer. My brother William Jr. used to encourage Little Will and I to take sips. It tasted sour-bitter and made my stomach sick and my nose stuffy as soon as it hit the back of my throat.

He would laugh and say,

"That's it, have another sip! It makes you big and strong."

At which point, his eldest son, Little Will

would hold the can with both hands and try to please his daddy by taking a long swallow without making a face.

Benji would watch his big brother, and almost as soon as he could walk, he would reach for his daddy's beer can. William Jr. would oblige both his sons when Hope wasn't around.

One afternoon last summer at the Cape, when Hope was out with the boys, I walked in on my brother and Hope's brother Larry sitting in the living room, talking about flying airplanes while listening to Billy Joel's *The Stranger* album.

Both men had their feet up on the antique coffee table. Empty bottles and cans of beer and bare feet on mahogany.

Laughing William Jr. held out his beer to me and said,

"Hey Beth, I'll give you ten dollars if you drink the rest of this."

"What?" Larry said laughing, "She's just a kid. Man, don't do that to her."

"We've done this before," my brother said to Larry, "but I've never seen her drink *ten* dollars' worth."

I remembered the gross taste from the first time, and I turned away and started to leave the room.

Then he said,

"Wait, you're going to turn down ten dollars? OK, make it twenty!"

I kept walking with his words at my back,

"Not even for *twenty* bucks? Or are you *really* just that much of a *baby*?"

I was used to George and Lydia always calling me a baby, but not him. Never him.

I turned around, walked towards his grinning face. He held out the can and I took it. I finished it in three gulps including his backwash.

Almost immediately, my nose stuffed up and the curdling in my stomach crawled up under my jaw.

I ran into the front hall guest bathroom, and wretched it all up.

"It's your fault for getting sick," he said walking in behind me while I had my head in the toilet.

"I didn't think you'd really take me up on it. Go to your room and wash-up. Don't tell Hope about this. It'll be our little secret."

He shut the door on his way out.

When everything was out and the dry heaves finally stopped, I stood up and flushed the toilet. There was a twenty-dollar bill left by the faucet.

✳ ✳ ✳

The fat man holding the red and white can yells again over his shoulder, and a rail thin, tall boy wearing a black leather jacket exits the house and walks towards the bus slow.

The man slaps the boy hard on the back of his head using the beer can. Beer jumps out of the can and onto the boy's hair and jacket.

The boy walks up the steps of the bus, turns to the old man,

"Hey!" he yells and flips off the old man with both hands.

The bus door closes.

Walking towards the back of the bus, he casually wipes beer from the back of his head.

His open jacket reveals a thin undershirt and worn Wrangler jeans with no belt. A skinny version of the man who just hit him.

He catches me staring and slows his walk to make lingering eye contact with me. I smell the spilt beer on him. He stops long enough as if he might sit next to me.

I turn to look out the window, then his heavy boots continue where he is welcomed by cheers and swears from the other boys already on the bus.

"Hell yeaaaah, Tommmaaaayyyyy!"

The sound of hands meeting in high-five slaps.

"Fuck yer old man," yells another.

"Someday I will knock him down," an angry voice says, "I will hit that bastard so hard; he won't never get up."

I look up at the bus driver's mirror, he is watching the rowdy boys in the back. *Would the bus driver protect me?*

Since that first ride with my dad years ago when I was little, I rode the city bus many times.

I tried to recall my feelings of confidence doing that trip to school by myself year after year in Providence. This felt more wild, more dangerous than a crowded city bus full of adult strangers.

The bus became noisier with each person that got on, and luckily, the seat next to me was still empty. *Thank God.*

Daylight now, shapes and details of scenery become more visible.

Where am I?

Everything is different.

And I have no instruments to tell me.

* * *

Hope's brother, Larry, owned a small plane, and my brother, William Jr., wanted to learn how to fly it. Larry was showing my brother, me and the kids his aviation books and talking about his adventures flying to the Virgin Islands. The conversation became technical when he described how flying a plane is much different than driving a car.

"Pitch, yaw and roll," Larry explained, "are the three ways a plane can move during flight."

Larry held out his forearm and hand flat as if his fingertips were the nose of the plane and his elbow the tail.

"A plane can point its nose up or down, that's what we call pitch. It can turn left or right, that's called yaw. Or it can roll and even fly upside down. Fighter pilots do all three at hundreds of miles per hour!"

"That's cool Uncle Larry," my nephew Little Will said.

"But what if you are up in the clouds," I said, "and you can't see where you are going?"

"That's why your brother will have to study very hard. A pilot must learn how to read the instruments and rely on them to tell him where he's going. You could be off by just one degree in any direction, and you might not know it until it's too late."

"Too late?"

"Yeah. Too late," Larry said as he made a crashing sound and demonstrated a plane crash with his hand doing a nose-dive into the table.

* * *

On the bus that morning, I search for ways to orient myself in this big unfurling pattern of the unfamiliar:

Trees.
Granite rocks.
Road.
Double yellow line.
Potholes.
Guard rail.
Dented guardrail.
Trees.
Granite.

Dirt driveway.
Rusted car on cement blocks.
Trailer.
Rusted metal chair.
Woodpile.
Road.
Pothole.
Mailbox.
Driveway.
House.
Barking dog.
Wooden shed with roof half gone.
Dented mailbox.
Trailer.
Barking dog chained to a tree.

I don't look at the people getting on the bus. I don't want to make eye contact.

The bus is full of all types of chatter, laughter, and some occasional swearing and yelling.

The driver slows down in what seems the middle of nowhere. The bus has reached the end of Rattlesnake Road.

Stop sign.

Hill to our right with a single house perched on the slope of it. A white clapboard house with a single line of smoke curling up from the chimney.

No driveway, no cars.

No mailbox.

The bus driver leans over towards an 8-track tape player mounted under the dash next to his right knee. He presses the large plastic rectangle tape into the player and turns the knob.

The hard guitar of AC/DC pipes through small speakers mounted on the wall of the bus on either side of his rear-view mirror.

The driver looks back at his riders and turns up the volume loud enough to drown out the yelling and swearing.

The Mickey Mouse watch Joy gave me for my sixth-grade birthday tells me it's 7:15 as we turn onto a main road and the bus goes faster.

I miss her and Maggie and Susan.

It all happened so fast.

Tears form in my throat. The muscles under my jawbone twinge.

God no, not here.

I cannot cry here.

Stop it. Just stop!

Staring out the window, the scenery blurs, and I escape into the movie in my mind.

The happy movie of Hope and Little Will; white sand and clear blue skies.

Warmth. I crave it.

The warmth of last summer.

The warmth of Christmases with Little Will.

The warmth of Hope's hugs and Benji's laughter.

I want more dinosaurs, more snow angels.

I feel the sensation of someone's eyes on me. I face forward to discover a small face with big eyes staring at me from over the top of the seat in front of me.

A young girl.

I smile, she laughs.

Keeping her eyes right on mine, she lifts her hand to her face, her fingernails blackened with dirt. Her hands reminded me of characters from a Dickens novel. Still looking at me she sticks her finger inside her nose and roots around. I look out the window at the dense trees along the road.

That two-foot-high dented metal guardrail could not stop this bus from going over the edge.

I heard a loud laugh, and when I look back at her, she proudly shows me the prize bounty of boogers stacked on her index finger. Laughing she wipes it on the top of the seat. Then she turns around and sits down leaving her prize in front of me.

Ugh, gross, why don't I have a Kleenex. Mom says to always carry Kleenex.

The sound of the boys in the back was getting louder, and the driver turned up the music to distortion.

Sound creates an invisible wall.

The bus rattles and vibrates loud.

AC/DC's *Highway to Hell* grinds into my skull while I ride on a bus with people I don't know to a place I've never been.

WHAT'S IN
A NAME?

I t's now 7:50 AM. I stop in the front office to ask directions to the registrar. A woman with big hair twice the size of her head, wearing an oversized flannel shirt looks at me from behind the counter.

"Freshman?"

"Yes ma'am. Could you please tell me where I need to go for my class schedule and textbooks?"

Her eyes look me up and down, without any effort to try hiding it.

"You're new to these parts are ya?"

"Yes ma'am," I say.

"Where from?"

My stomach tightens. After the long bus ride, I

needed to pee, and I just wanted to get my schedule.

She asks again. This time with a smile,

"Where *are* you *from?*"

"Rhode Island."

"Ahhh," she nods her head up and down, "A flatlander."

She speaks in a voice that I will soon learn is the New Hampshire accent.

"Flatlander?"

"Yeah," her head lowered now and eyes on me over the top of her 1950s cat-eye frames.

"What's a flatlander?"

"That's you kiddo. Someone who ain't from around these parts."

Waving her arm in a sweeping gesture towards the space behind me, she says,

"These kids all know each other since they were wearin' diapers. Grew up together. Go to church together, celebrate Christmases and Fourth of July together. Families been here for generations."

I look up at the clock above on the wall behind her, it's already 8:00.

"Can you give me my class schedule. Please."

"What's your name, sweetheart?"

"Beth Lawrence," I say shifting my weight from left to right, and back again, wishing I had looked for the bathroom first.

She runs her finger down a piece of paper on the clipboard, licks her thumb, lifts the corner of the paper, and looks at the next page.

"No Beth Lawrence listed here."

"We just moved here a few weeks ago, didn't my parents call?"

"That wouldn't be me honey, you'd have to talk to someone else about that. I'm the school nurse and handle the Freshman registration once a year. That's all."

Am I at the wrong school?

Did my father put me on the wrong bus?

She looks at me for a long time, and then over my shoulder at the line of people growing behind me.

"I got other customers waitin' Sweetheart."

I lean over the counter trying to see the list of names myself. She raises the clipboard up to her chest.

Her fingers tight sausages, a thin gold band on her ring finger looks too snug to ever take off.

"Are you sure there is no Beth Lawrence?"

"Who?"

"Beth Lawrence," I say realizing how seldom I say my name.

"It's my name, isn't there a Beth Lawrence listed there?"

"Nope, don't see none," she said.

Then it occurs to me.

"Is there *anyone* listed with a last name of Lawrence?"

She looks down the list again and lifts up the paper,

"Nope I don't see – oh, now, wait a minute. I see here a Hope Lawrence."

"That's it," I say relieved, "that's me."

She looks at me suspiciously over the top of her glasses again,

"You just said your name is Beth."

"Yes, it is. I mean, I go by my middle name, Elizabeth."

"Says here, *Hope*."

"Right, I know. That's my first name, Hope. I go by my middle name."

"But you told me Beth. That's different than Elizabeth," she said, the wrinkles around her pursed lips deepen.

"Beth is my nickname, short for Elizabeth," I said.

I hate being called Beth.

At my private school this never came up because I had been there so long I never had to explain it. They called me Beth from my first day in nursery school.

I rarely if ever even said my name, and when I did, I didn't like saying it. It sounded harsh to me and felt strange in my mouth.

And even more, I hated having to explain it.

My face hot. My feet and hands cold.

Big hair lady grins big.

She must see that I am blushing.

She places the clipboard down on the counter so I can't see it and walks a few feet over to a green metal desk with a cardboard box on top of it.

She fingers through the box and pulls a card out, inspects it carefully with her glasses on, then pulls them down and looks at me again. They hang around her neck on a black lanyard resting on her ample flannel chest.

She puts the card down, opens the desk drawer and pulls out a stick of gum. She slowly unwraps it. A flash of lime green paper and foil.

Wrigley's spearmint. She presses the wrapper between the tips of her fingers and flicks it into the metal trash can next to the desk.

A girl's voice from far behind me yells out,

"C'mon Carol, it'll be Christmas before you get to us!"

"Oh, hold your horses! We got us a flatlander here and *as usual* they gotta *do things different* than we do."

Murmuring swells behind me.

Hot sweat pools in my armpits.

Did I put my deodorant on today?

❊ ❊ ❊

Wearing deodorant was a new habit I started that summer at the Cape. One night when Hope was brushing my hair, she explained to me about how our body changes in puberty.

Now that you are becoming a woman, your body will experience many changes. You may sweat more, and sometimes you will smell different. Not bad, just different, and from now on, you should always wear it. Every day.

The very next day Hope bought some for me and showed me how to correctly apply it.

❊ ❊ ❊

The woman returns to the counter and looks at me again before handing me the card.

"These are your classes," she says, "but it says here your name is Hope Lawrence, not Elizabeth and certainly not Beth."

Just as I reach for the card, she pulls it back.

"How do I know this is you?"

I am flummoxed at this point. I have to pee, and I want to cry.

She grins big, pops her gum between her teeth, hands me the schedule card and says,

"Welcome to the next four years of your life! First period starts at 8:15. If you get lost, just ask the other students where things are. I'm sure they will be happy to tell *you* where to go."

"Thank you" I said with my manners on autopilot, "nice to meet you, Carol."

I turn and walk by a long line of people, and I hear Carol say,

"Damn flatlanders, they move up here and act like they own the place."

Shamed and embarrassed by this woman, I take her rudeness and heap it on myself more.

I walk down the grey-tiled corridor along the

banks of lockers looking for locker number 278.

She didn't believe me.

She hates my name.

Beth.

I hate my name.

I think I forgot my deodorant.

I must stink.

I get all the way to the end of the gray hall and realize that locker 278 is *upstairs.* I notice a wooden door that says "Girls" and hurry in.

The bathroom cement walls painted gray with black stalls and thick, block-glass windows just below the ceiling. I'd held it so long, my body took forever to pee, and my brain escaped to better places.

❄ ❄ ❄

At my old school the first day of the term was extra special. Every year in fall and spring, first through eighth grade, we received a book list, and we would all go get our books at the school bookstore next to the gym building. It would be an event: well organized and timed for each class to get new fresh books, fresh notebooks and new pens and pencils.

In eighth grade mom told me I was mature enough to get a fancy pen like my sister Lydia had. So, in addition to my usual supply of blue BIC sticks and Paper Mate Flair markers, I picked out a fountain pen. It looked similar to the one my sister brought back from Paris, very modern, sleek and colorful.

I thought it was so cool how Lydia always had blue ink stains on her right index and middle fingers when she came to the dinner table after she did her homework. Her pen from Paris was red with a sterling silver top.

The one I picked out was forest green, the same color as my favorite school sweater. It wasn't from Paris, and it had a plastic not silver cap, but it was a real fountain pen, like Lydia's. The bookstore clerk showed me how to refill it and how to write with it so as to not crush the nib.

I loved that fountain pen, and I loved how I felt writing with it.

* * *

My fountain pen was safe at home in my new bedroom. Now without any books or notebooks, this didn't feel like I was in a school at all. It was something else.

I looked at my watch and thought of Joy and Susan and Maggie, they would likely be done getting their new books and school supplies by now.

I smelled smoke and realized I was done peeing and had been just sitting there. I flushed and washed my hands, ignoring the two girls leaning against the wall sharing a cigarette under windows that don't open.

The school was two floors of gray on the inside. Gray lockers, and gray painted floors where there was no gray asbestos tile flooring or linoleum.

The top half of every door to the classrooms was glass so you could see in, with the room number painted on the wood just above it.

Freshman English, my first class, was at the other end of the hall from where my locker was.

Maybe they just don't have books in public school?

I walk into a room cluttered with single arm molded plastic desks with metal legs.

Every one of the desks was made for right handers. I am left-handed.

I walk all the way to the back and sit in the farthest corner by the window. I keep my eyes down.

Self-conscious from my encounter with the registrar lady, I become acutely aware of sweat under my arms and worry that I must stink by now. I did not have any breakfast besides orange juice. It was too early for breakfast when dad woke me at 5:15 AM.

The wall of windows looks out over the parking lot and beyond that I see a track and what must be the football field. Tall trees everywhere.

My dad used to share stories about how he taught orienteering at camp when he was a teenage boy. He learned how to find his way out of dense wilderness just by having a compass and a map.

That first morning of school in a new state, I didn't even know where the sun was.

The sky was just a lighter shade of gray than the walls inside the school.

The classroom fills up quickly with students who seem friendly and comfortable with each other.

A large man with a huge belly that spills over his jeans, a bright red beard and a receding hairline walks in behind them with a big smile.

"Hello Freshman! Welcome to Freshman English!"

He hangs his leather coat on the back of his chair.

"My name is Mr. McG. You can call me Jimbo when and *if* I get to know ya. But until I say so, it's Mr. McG to you."

"I just moved here," he said with a strong accent,

"I'm from New York City. What you guppies affectionately call a city boy. Or my favorite colloquialism you like to use, a flatlander."

The bell rang. 8:15.

He leaned against the front of his desk, crossing his arms and legs in front of him, he continued,

"Let me be clear, I don't give a rat's ass what you think of me, just that you do your assignments and come to class. Got that?"

With his wire-rimmed glasses, thick full beard

and round belly, he seemed to me a red-headed version of Santa Claus, except, maybe not as friendly.

His eyes did a quick sweep of the room, then he said,

"Ok guppies, let's do roll call."

He rolled up the sleeves of his faded, blue Oxford shirt. It was just like the ones my brother George wore; except George usually wore a tie with his Oxford shirts.

"I think that's what this is," he said, reaching for the clipboard behind him on his desk.

He walked over to his leather jacket and took something from the inside pocket. Then resumed his position leaning against the front of the battered wooden desk facing us.

"James Allen,"

A thin, tall dirty blond-haired boy three rows back from the front raised his hand,

"Hee-ya," James Allen said.

The girls around him giggled at just the sound of him saying his name.

Boys.

Oh my God, boys!

I'm in school with BOYS!

The girls giggled; James tossed his bangs back. That's how he would get his hair out of his face, never with his hands, but with a casual sweeping toss of his head, and of course they fell right back down perfectly over his eyes.

"Peter Allen."

"Yep."

"Pamela Beech?"

"Here."

"Maria …"

As he called the names, I looked at the people around me for the first time.

Boys and girls, every single one of them Caucasian and all dressed pretty much the same. All wearing jeans or corduroys.

Some girls wore clogs, but most of the ones I could see wore Nike Cortez sneakers. White with a red swoosh.

The boys wore black Nike Cortez sneakers with the white swoosh or black Converse high tops. Some boys had on flannel shirts, and some girls did too. Two other girls had wool sweaters similar to mine with the Fair Isle yoke pattern at the shoulders.

The main difference was the hair. All the girls had one of three hair styles. The Dorothy Hamill cut. The long straight and pulled back with a headband or some type of shoulder-length feathered style with bangs. And some of the boys had longer hair than the girls.

They looked like one big extended family. They looked like they were all related.

The Peanut's comic strip drone of wa-wa, wa-wa-wa-wa finally cleared when I heard, "Hope Lawrence?"

I raised my hand silently, as I was taught to do in class always before speaking.

"Here," I said.

The teacher continued, "Bill Littlefield –"

Before I realized what I was doing, my hand went up again, "Mr. McG?"

"Yes," he said.

"I'm sorry, but my name is Beth."

"Says here Hope. You can fix that after class with the downstairs office," he said and looked back down at his clipboard.

"Bill Little - "

"Here."

At my old school we were taught to clarify things as early as possible to avoid misunderstanding.

I raised my hand again certain that my face was beet red by now.

"Excuse me, Mr. McG?"

"Yes, Hope. "

Now the whole class turned around.

"I'm sorry, it's just that I go by my middle name, Beth."

"Says here Hope, isn't that correct?"

"Yes, sir. That's correct. Hope is my first name."

"Why don't you go by your first name?"

His question hung in the air.

It was such a simple question, and yet one I had never been asked and did not know the answer to.

"I've always been called Beth," I said.

He started to write on the sheet and said, "OK, Hope Beth Lawrence."

I winced.

Just drop it.

But it was so ingrained in me to *set the record straight* as my father always liked to say.

"No, it's..."

A murmur went through the room

What am I doing?? Just drop it.

"I mean, I'm sorry, my middle name is Elizabeth."

"Elizabeth, that was my mother's name," Mr. McG said, "such a pretty name, why don't you go by Elizabeth then?"

Why have I never asked myself this question? I had never been called Hope, and I always liked Elizabeth much better.

I adored my 7th and 8th grade French teacher. She always called me Elizabeth in French class, and it sounded so pretty when she said it.

With her delicate French accent, it sounded like "Elizabett."

I always felt pretty in French class.

Mr. McG repeated his question,

"So why don't you go by Elizabeth?"

The class was silent with all eyes on me now. Suddenly the boys looked so intimidating.

"I just never have, except for in French class," I said.

"We haven't had French class yet, that's tomorrow," said the blonde girl next to James Allen.

James Allen had turned his whole body around and straddled his long denim legs around the back of the chair. James Allen was looking right through me. I could see light blue eyes through those haystack blond bangs he kept flicking back.

"I had French last year," I said.

Mr. McG put the clipboard down on the desk behind him; stood up from his leaning position and took a step towards me.

"You're new here aren't ya?"

"Yes sir," I said.

He took another step in my direction.

"Where from?"

"Rhode Island."

He was standing in the aisle now right next to James Allen.

"How many years of French have you had, kid?"

Don't you ever lie to me, young lady. Never. Ever.

"Uh, five or six... I guess?"

I could feel myself shrinking in my seat.

I wanted to disappear or climb out the window behind me.

Half-breaths make you invisible.

I kept my eyes locked on Mr. McG, too terrified to look at James Allen or any other of the eyes on me.

"Private school?"

"Yes sir."

"A snob!" came a voice from the other side of the room.

More laughter.

My face hot my feet and hands were ice.

"Preppy snob no doubt," said a boy from the front of the room.

"No," Mr. McG said, holding up his hand, "no, no. We don't know if she's a snob, but she is *definitely* a flatlander."

Then Mr. McG took a few more steps. He was even bigger up-close. He stood one desk away, and towering over me he asked,

"Ok, Miss Hope Elizabeth Lawrence, tell us, if you go by your middle name, why don't you go by Elizabeth, instead of Beth?"

People were getting restless; bodyweight shifting in the tiny orange plastic chairs. Sneakers and boots on asbestos tiled floor. My arm pits were melting, and I was starting to feel sweat everywhere even in my crotch. *Oh, God no, please don't let it be my period.* I had forgotten to count my days with the move and everything I could not even remember when I was due.

"OK, let's try this: do you know who decided to call you Beth?"

He crossed his arms and rested them on his Santa-sized belly. This close his arms were huge, the sleeves of his blue Oxford shirt rolled up and his forearms covered in thick curly red hair. My eyes went to my hands on my desk.

I felt like I was going to cry.

I hate the name Beth. I never liked it; it sounds so ugly.

The man in front of me was a teacher – an authority figure. *Don't you ever lie to me, young lady.*

I could taste Ivory Soap on my tongue.

He asked a question that in fourteen years, I had never asked myself.

"I don't know," I said quietly to the desk.

Mr. McG heard me and said, "You don't know?"

Laughter broke out.

James Allen said with his thick New Hampshire accent, "You don't know who named ya?"

"That's *wicked* hilarious," said the blonde girl next to him.

She wore a gingham button up shirt. Her shiny hair shaped in a Dorothy Hamill bob.

"Don't you have parents," she asked.

More laughter.

Mr. McG unfolded his arms and lifted his thick butcher block hands up to the students.

"Ok, gang, that's enough. Calm down, fun's over."

He walked back to the front of the class, "You can thank - Beth - here later when I give you your homework assignment."

He went through the rest of the roll call and there were no further interruptions.

Is this what public school will be like?

It was bad enough being put on the spot in elementary school math drills where the teacher would hold an equation card up and point at us to stand and recite the answer. That was anxiety inducing, but this was worse.

This was way worse. He was not testing my knowledge of math multiplication tables; he was testing me. He was questioning who I was. Publicly humiliated, for just asking to be called the name I had been called for years.

It was like that horrible Sunday School class where I got in trouble for asking why it was only Jesus and his father in heaven and not his mother too. I looked around the room for closet doors. *Would Mr. McG ever lock me in a closet like the Sunday School teacher did?*

I felt smaller in my seat. *I don't even know why I am called Beth.*

When he finished taking attendance, he put his clipboard back on the desk and started to screw the cap back on his fountain pen.

"Well, now we know about one of your classmates, and trust me, this term you will all get to know each other much better than you do now. But first let me tell you a little bit about myself."

His big hands made the pen look much smaller than it was.

He held the pen out in front of himself and looked at it for a long time. He was left-handed like me.

"This pen," he wagged it next to the left side of his head, "used to belong to Allen Ginsberg. Does anyone know who that is?"

I knew that name. I had heard it mentioned several times in conversations between George, Kate and Lydia. I knew that he was a poet they liked, but I did not dare raise my hand again.

"He is the Walt Whitman of this century," Mr.

McG said, "One of the great modern Beat poets that we will be studying. He wrote a poem called *Howl.* Which you will be pleased to know we will be reading this term, and you may even have to memorize parts of it to recite it. It was he, the great Beat Poet, and my dear friend, Allen Ginsberg, who gave me this pen."

With hands at his sides now, he began to pace back and forth in front of his desk.

The way he held that pen made me think of Lenny from Steinbeck's *Of Mice And Men.* His thick, fleshy fist could snap it in two.

"Like I said, I am from *the* city. Not a city but the city. For there is only *one* city. New York. I lived in the village. And Allen Ginsberg gave me this pen. You don't deserve to hear the whole story today, guppies, because you won't appreciate it."

He held the pen up again wagging it at us,

"After we read *Howl* by Ginsberg, and *Leaves of Grass* by Whitman, as a Christmas present to all of you, I will tell you the story of me and Allen. Allen and me, and you will *never* forget it. And the lines of *Howl* will be forever etched in your hearts."

He walked over behind his desk, lifted his leather jacket off the back of the chair and put the pen in the inside pocket.

"New York. Who's been there?"

He looked at me, "Beth, have you been there?"

"No sir," I said.

Heads looked around the room.

Zero hands went up.

Holding his jacket with its back facing us, he held it up squarely by the shoulders so we could clearly see the back of it.

He nodded his head.

"See that gash in the leather down there?"

We all looked. A diagonal slash with edges curled open in the leather. He shook the jacket up and down and said,

"This is New York, this is life in the Village."

James Allen shifted in his chair and leaned forward, and asked in his cracking voice,

"What happened?"

"I got mugged. At knifepoint. Asshole wanted my wallet and my kidney. He got my fist instead."

The boys sat-up taller and leaned in.

One girl in the front reached for his coat, he walked towards her and let her finger the opening.

"It goes all the way through," she said with excitement in her voice.

"Yep. This coat saved my life," he said, walking back behind the desk, he hung it carefully on the back of the chair.

"New York. It's the only city worth knowing. Except for maybe, Paris."

The bell rang and everyone started to get up.

"Hold-on," he said, "Hold-on, Guppies."

Everyone froze. He had won them over; he had commanded them.

"For your first assignment – you will write me a 300-word essay on your name. Who named you? Where did it come from? Is it a family name? What are your nicknames etc. etc."

He looked right at me.

"And, most importantly, what do you think about your name? Due tomorrow!"

The scraping sound of the small metal feet of the non-desk-desks and groans filled the air.

I pulled my folded-up schedule out of my pocket to see where I needed to go next. Biology, Room 110. Downstairs again but I didn't know where it was exactly, and I had to find a bathroom.

The possibility of having started my period sent a wash of anxiety through me. I waited until almost everyone was up and near the door out before I stood up. I looked at the plastic orange seat where I had been. Every young girl's nightmare is to bleed through her clothes in school.

I walked quickly towards the door, Mr. McG said,

"Hey, kid."

"Yes sir?"

"Don't worry. I'm a flatlander too, and you know what? I think you're tougher than you realize."

"Thank you, sir."

As I stepped into the hall, I realized that was the first time I had ever left a class empty-handed.

Even in Kindergarten I often had some piece of art to take home that we had made during the day. I started having books and hours of homework from first grade onward. I loved books and notebooks, and homework, and this felt weird.

No syllabus, no books.

What is this place?

Five minutes to find a bathroom again, get some water from the bubbler, and get to my next class.

In the bathroom I was so happy that it wasn't my period, but I was sweating from everywhere.

I was so used to wearing my school uniform skirt, and sitting on cool, wooden chairs at a regular desk, that wearing corduroys twisted into tiny plastic right-arm desks as a left-hander was going to be an adjustment.

In the hallway between classes, I passed one girl wearing a skirt instead of pants. She had on a caramel-colored corduroy skirt with a flowery top and a sheer black cardigan sweater. Unlike the other girls who were mostly dressed just like the boys, she stood out.

Downstairs I saw one very tall girl with long red hair wearing overalls with a pink short-sleeve top. She had long hair down to her waist pulled back in a matching pink ribbon. The front pocket of her overalls held a row of pens and pencils. A group of five girls surrounded her as they walked together down the hallway. I wondered if she was like Anne, Miriam or Kathy. I hoped she was nice like Joy, Susan and Maggie.

I got into Biology before the bell rang, but the class was full. A room of windows and lab tables with four chairs at each table.

The teacher looked at me and said,

"Why don't you take that empty seat back there? Oh, and here, take these," he said pointing to a blue hardcover textbook, and a workbook on the table in front of his desk.

The textbook was blue with *Biology* written in white lettering on the spine.

The cover was so dirty, and the previous owner had inked in all the letters except for the B, the O, and the Y. The corners were bent and worn exposing their cardboard interior. The workbook looked new. I walked to the back of the room to the only empty chair.

I watched my feet navigate my way until,

"Well hello again," a voice cracked.

It was James Allen and the girl who had been sitting next to him in English class with another blonde girl I didn't recall seeing before.

"Hi," I said, and sat down on the metal folding chair making myself as small as possible. At least the seat was cool compared to the plastic ones in English class. Behind me was a gray cement block wall with an empty cork bulletin board bolted to the wall.

Always sit with your back to the wall.

The teacher was an old man in his fifties or sixties with short gray hair cut close, military style.

He already had chalk on his face and the only thing written on the board was his name *Mr. Fisk*, and the name of the class, *Biology* both written in large, neat, cursive lettering.

The bell rang. Mr. Fisk took the piece of paper and while seated behind his desk started to take roll call.

"James Allen"

"Hee ya," said James Allen.

Mr. Fisk looked towards our table and made a checkmark on the paper.

"Mr. Fisk?"

"Yes, James?"

Although it was the very first day of high school for all of us, it seemed everyone already knew James Allen, even the teachers.

With his eyes on the teacher, James pointed to me.

"To save you time, this here's Beth Lawrence. She's new."

"Oh?"

Mr. Fisk looked confused.

He looked down at his list.

"You won't see it on there, ya see, I'm just trying to save you some time."

A boy at the next table added laughing,

"And a lot of pain."

James continued, "On the paper there it says Hope Lawrence, but she *prefers* that you call her Beth. Which she will tell you is a nickname for her full middle name Elizabeth."

The class laughed uproariously, but Mr. Fisk seemed puzzled and then irritated by what James was talking about. He waved his hand for James to be quiet and continued to read down the list.

When he got to my name, he called out Hope Lawrence, looked at James, then said, "Oh, right."

He wrote something down on the page, and then went on with roll.

After taking attendance, he gave us a short lecture, and then assigned us to read pages 1-5 in the textbook and to answer the questions on pages 1-3 in the workbook.

I took what little bit of comfort and familiarity I could from the simple act of opening a text-book. Even if it was not crisp and new and said B O Y on it instead of BIOLOGY, I got to work reading the assignment.

The pages were marked up and someone had turned the number 1 of "Chapter 1" into an erect penis and had drawn hairy balls at the bottom of it.

I started reading the assignment while James and the girls started to talk about football, soccer and cheerleading tryouts. The students at other tables were talking too.

I focused on the assignment. It was so easy, all stuff I already knew. I remembered having learned about photosynthesis the same year I read *Silent Spring* by Rachel Carson. That was three years ago, in 6th grade science which I loved and had such a crush on the teacher. He was the only male teacher I'd ever taken a class with before today.

James Allen and the two girls I was sitting with did not seem at all concerned with the assignment.

Mr. Fisk sat behind his desk with his head down barely moving; maybe he was reading or even dozing off.

Apparently, I had sat at the table with the star jocks: James Allan played football; his girlfriend Jeanne had been skiing since she could walk; and her best friend Kim a petite girl with thick long blond hair was apparently also on the ski team.

They had not even opened the workbooks.

Kim turned to me and said,

"Hey Beth, so are you going to try out for any sports?"

"I'm not sure," I said, "I live pretty far away."

"That's ok," she said, "there are second buses to take everyone home in the evening after practice. Sports are very big here. Everyone is on a team. That is, unless you're a druggie or something."

The bell rang.

On the way out the teacher collected the workbooks and said, "If you haven't finished your work, you may take it home, otherwise please leave the workbooks on my desk so I can review your answers tonight."

I noticed that James and his girlfriend Jeanne left their workbooks at the front even though they had not answered any of the questions.

At lunchtime, I followed the crowd into the cafeteria. It was a large open room with windows on two sides; a stage at the opposite end of the room from where the lunch line and kitchen were located. Long, rectangular tables with welded metal benches made the tables and benches one unit.

I would give anything to be at my old school now having lunch with Joy, Susan and Maggie.

I imagined how they would be laughing and eating in the nice dining hall with lots of windows, pleasant lighting, indigo carpet, and round wooden tables with individual wooden chairs.

I took a tray and got in line. Everything looked the same – tan tray, white rolls, white mashed potatoes, and light gray gravy. Hot dogs were at the end of the line served by a stout woman with a big head of hair under her hair net.

"One dog or two?"

"One please."

"Relish or ketchup?"

"Relish, please."

She eyed me up and down as she tucked relish alongside the bare hotdog on my plate.

I took my tray to a table by the windows. I liked sitting with my back to a wall, whenever possible.

* * *

Never sit with your back exposed. I learned that one the hard way from my brother George and also from Anne, Miriam and Kathy at my old school who all used to sneak up behind me to scare me.

In the case of George, it was always worse than scare me.

One summer at my grandfather's picnic table, George walked up behind me, put his big hands on my small shoulders and pressed his groin into the back of my head and neck.

His belt buckle digging into the top of my head. I tried to get away, but he had strong hands that could snap my collar bone if he wanted to.

"Don't disappoint me Beth, or I'll make you play fifty-two card pick-up later. You little brat, if you don't do as I say..."

He started to laugh, placed his hands on either side of my head right under my ears and started to twist me towards him.

"Beth, you must kiss the belt of King Arthur," he commanded.

"No!"

I pulled my body weight down hard enough to escape his grip and slip my body under the picnic table.

My ears, neck and jaw hurt so bad. It felt like he twisted my neck so much that it pulled my ears right off my head. I checked my ears. No blood. Just ringing on one side. I got some splinters on the back of my upper left thigh from sliding so fast under the table.

George's Top Siders and khakis moved away as Grandma and mom approached.

Mom's face appeared under the table,

"Young lady, for heaven's sake, what are you doing under there?"

George was gone, and I began to crawl out on my hands and knees.

"Careful," mom said, "You'll get grass stains on your pretty dress."

Grandpa walked towards us from the house and said, "What is Beth doing under the table?"

Then he scolded my mother, "You must teach your daughter some manners. She's a young lady, not a dog begging for scraps."

Grandma brushed the freshly cut grass off my dress and smoothed my hair. "Oh, she's fine. Let's have some fresh corn from the garden and some chicken. Where's your brother, dear?"

"I just passed him on my way out here," Grandpa said, "He said he had to use the bathroom, and to start without him."

* * *

I couldn't get my cardboard milk carton open when I heard a voice say,

"Those are such a pain, I know."

A girl with shoulder length brown hair pulled back with a wide plastic headband like mine stood in front of me smiling.

"OK if I sit here?"

She had a smile that crinkled the corners of her eyes, a round happy face that reminded me of Benji, my youngest nephew.

"Yes, please, sit down," I said.

"My name's Patty," she said and held out her hand.

I wiped the milk off my thumb and shook her hand.

"Nice to meet you," I said, "Beth Lawrence."

She pulled everything off her tray and put the tray on the bench beside her.

"So how do you like it so far?"

"Ah...well, I keep getting lost."

"Oh, you'll get used to it. I only know my way around because my mom works here."

"She does? What does she teach?"

"No," Patty said, "she's over there."

Patty pointed to the line of women behind the lunch counter and the heavyset woman with the big hair in the hair net who served me relish waved at us.

"That's my mom," Patty said.

Smiling, she waved back to her mom.

I waved a short, shy hello.

"So, what happened to you in English class this morning. You really just moved here?"

"Yeah, from Rhode Island,"

"You really are a flatlander."

She laughed, but not in a mean way.

"Everyone keeps saying that," I said, "what do they mean?"

"It just means you're not from here. You see we all grew up together and know each other pretty well. See those girls over there?"

She pointed to the blonde girl from English class and another blonde girl at the same table who was slightly taller.

"They are twins," she said, "and they're also cousins with James Allen, of course you know who he is."

"Yes," I said, "I noticed him."

"Who doesn't? He's so cute."

She pointed to a short heavy-set guy who looked totally different.

"But see that guy with the glasses, across from James Allen? That is his twin brother, Peter."

"Twins? They look totally different."

"Yeah, fraternal twins. There are four sets of them in our class alone. Anyway, our families have known each other for centuries. Kind of incestuous if you ask me. I certainly don't want to marry my third cousin. That's for damned sure."

She laughed, took a bite of her buttered white roll and while chewing, she continued,

"A flatlander is generally from south of here. Far south, like Boston or in your case, Rhode Island. Our teacher Mr. McG, he's a flatlander from Manhattan; and then there's a guy in our class who moved here last year, Steven. We all call him 'Stephan' with those shiny gorgeous locks of his. He's rich like you, but he's from Boston. His dad is a professor at Harvard and moved up here to write some big important book. His sister is really nice, but she was only here for a week. Then they sent her off to some fancy, private school somewhere down in Southern New Hampshire. Stephan skips class all the time. I don't know how he graduated from 8th grade. A total stoner."

She pointed to the windows behind me. "There's a covered smoking area outside. He's probably out there right now."

I stood up to see out the window behind me. A dark curly-haired boy who looked like the one who got on the bus that morning, had one hand on a cigarette the other in his jacket pocket.

"The smoking area is for the teachers," she said, "but the students that smoke go out there too, nobody bothers with them anymore. They don't care. They would be happy to skip class and sit in detention all day every day. So finally, the teachers just gave up. And now all the smokers hang out together: teachers, students and even the maintenance guys.

* * *

Smoking. Miriam, Kathy, Anne and Paige brought cigarettes on the 7th grade field trip to Nantucket. They passed around a pack of Newport Menthols and got all the girls to smoke down on the beach. When the pack came around to me, I said no thanks and took a walk down the beach instead. I was the only one who didn't try it.

I didn't smoke with the girls that day or ever, but then a few months later I wondered why they did it, and as usual, my curiosity got the best of me.

I snuck one from my sister's room and tried it in the space behind our three-car garage. I wanted to see what all the fuss was about.

It was awful.

It made me feel light-headed and then immediately sick to my stomach. I didn't understand why people smoked, but Anne, Miriam, Kathy and Paige sure made it look super cool that day on the beach.

❋ ❋ ❋

"Do you smoke?" Patty asked.

"My dad used to when I was little, and I tried it once. Made me sick."

I took a bite of the mashed potatoes with the tan-gray gravy, swallowed and confessed to her,

"I am not used to going to school with boys."

"What," she laughed, "No boys? What kind of school doesn't have boys?"

"A private, all-girls school."

"Oh," she said, "I have heard of those. You really *are* a preppie aren't you."

"I guess... *maybe*?"

Preppie. I had always thought of my brother

George as the preppie because he attended one of the best prep schools in the world, and then went all Ivy, but I never thought of myself that way.

I was the girl who would not be a debutante. The girl who lost her best friend, Paige, for not being rich enough to be a debutante.

But here at this rural public school in 1979 New Hampshire, I was instantly seen as the rich one, the preppie, the snob. A flatlander from the big city.

"What's your favorite TV show?" Patty asked.

A flush of embarrassment warmed my face.

"We don't have a TV," I said.

She stopped peeling her orange.

"What?! No TV, who doesn't have a TV?"

"We used to have --"

Don't say that she already thinks you are rich. "My parents heard somewhere that TV is bad for you. Mom calls it the boob tube. So now we don't have one."

Patty laughed.

"Boob tube, that's funny. I don't know what kind of TV your parents were watching."

She handed me a section of her peeled orange, I took it, and it was sweet.

"Thank you," I said.

I was so anxious, hadn't even noticed any oranges in the lunch line.

"When you did have a TV," Patty asked, "what shows did you like to watch?"

"I liked Charlie's Angels and Wonder Woman."

Patty smiled, "Charlie's Angels. Which angel are you?"

"I always wanted to be Kelly," I said, "but my friends always insisted I play Sabrina."

"I wanted to be Kelly too! You must miss your friends," she said.

"I do..."

We both stared at what was left of our lunches.

"You could always come over and watch TV at my house," she said, cheerfully.

"Thank you, I would like that," I said, "but I live all the way out in Stapledown."

"Oh wow, that's way out in the boonies! Even for here."

After dinner that night, drying dishes while mom washed, I asked,

"Mom, where'd my name come from?"

"You were named after your great, great, great, aunt. Hope Elizabeth. She was a brilliant woman, and a teacher."

"Why do you call me Beth?"

"That was your brother's idea. George said 'Elizabeth' was too long to say, and when you were a baby, he watched after you a lot. He started calling you Beth. And soon we all called you that."

My throat tightened up. I started coughing.

❈ ❈ ❈

My whole body hated the name Beth, whenever I heard it, my body knew what I would not "officially know" for almost two decades hence in the *rubble of the big truth.*

It would be in the 1990s when George would be in town for a conference on the West Coast. I would not have seen him in years, but for some reason, he would get my number from mom and call to see if I'd meet him for dinner.

After dinner he would make a comment as casual and cheerful as if discussing good weather. He would laugh that awful laugh of his and say,

"Mom left you with me all the time. You always ate the cigarette butts out of the ashtray, and then you'd throw them up."

He would laugh.

"What? You let me eat cigarette butts? How old was I?"

"I dunno," he would say, "you were still in diapers."

By the time he told me this I would be an adult. I would have certain memories of what he'd done, but my brain heard his words with shock and disbelief.

Cognitive dissonance with the years of mom's declarations of how much my brother held me and loved me. How he looked after me and how kind he was to me when I was a baby. How his was the intellectual and character gold standard I would be held to and always trying to catch up to. Brilliant, perfect, George.

You let me eat cigarette butts and thought it was funny that I threw them up??

He would not explain.

He would not apologize.

He would only chuckle his laugh that my somatic memory knows so well.

Then he would say,

"You were so funny - you put everything in your mouth."

* * *

I couldn't stop coughing. It was like my throat was closing up.

"Are you alright, dear?"

"I'm fine," I said barely able to speak, "just got something stuck in my throat."

Mom took a clean, still-wet glass from the dry rack and filled it with water from the tap. I gulped it down taking only one breath.

"Thanks, mom," I said.

"I hope you're not getting sick. You know you always leave the house with wet hair in the morning. You're likely to catch a cold."

What just happened?

It took me a minute to calm down. I took a plate from the drying rack and wiped it slowly.

"So...mom, if my first name is Hope, why did you never call me that?"

"We already have one Hope in the family, dear,

William Jr.'s wife."

Hope married into the family years after I was born, this doesn't make sense.

"Hope is a pretty name. I like the name Hope. Could you try calling me Hope instead of Beth? It's what they have me listed as at school?"

"That will be too confusing dear. Especially at Christmas time. Besides, Hope is a bit of a large woman, you don't want to look like that do you?"

I thought Hope was beautiful, but mom always made a point of sharing her disapproval of the baby weight Hope didn't lose after Benji.

"Well how about Elizabeth, why don't we call me Elizabeth? That's what my French teacher called me. It sounds pretty, and I like it better than Beth."

"Beth, let's not make more changes right now dear, your father has enough on his mind."

"Can you try to call me Elizabeth, please?"

"I can try dear, if that's what you really want. I can try."

The next day in class I turned in my essay about being named after my great, great, great aunt who had been a teacher, and explained that it was my brother who started calling me Beth as a baby.

Mr. McG made us read them aloud in class after he gave them back, and when I got to the part about my much older brother calling me Beth because *Elizabeth was too long to say*, the class laughed, and Peter Allen said,

"I was born first by only three minutes, and I named my brother James. But he doesn't know that, do ya Jimmy?"

Mr. McG wrote a long comment next to the big red "A" on my paper that read,

You can change your name to whatever you want. Remember what I said to you on the first day, you're tougher than you realize.

Mom called me Elizabeth off and on for all of a week.

By the following weekend she forgot, and I got tired of reminding her and asking her to.

COLD DUCK

My French was advanced enough to place me into senior French. The class was smaller, only about 10 students including two junior year students and me.

Paul, a junior who sat next to me in class had a perfect smile and green eyes. He asked me out during our conversational exercises.

My parents wanted to 'screen' him, so mom suggested I invite him for dinner. My house was so far from school, but Paul was seventeen and had his driver's license, so he borrowed his mother's station wagon and made the trek all the way to my house. He would be my first dinner guest.

Mom cooked up a lovely dinner of steak, salad and green beans, and Paul said all the right things.

My parents both being all-Ivy, as soon as he said the word, "Yale", they treated him like part of the family.

Most students at my school didn't even go to college, so for someone to even apply to an Ivy League school was an event. If they got in and attended and graduated, their name would be enshrined in the same case with the jock trophies.

Paul was so handsome and seemed so mature, I just listened in awe as he said all the right things; he sounded so smart and confident with my parents.

During mom's delicious chocolate mousse dessert, I wanted to disappear when my father put down his fork, wiped his mouth with his linen napkin and asked,

"So Paul, what are your intentions with my daughter?"

"Well sir, I would like to date her."

Dad looked across the table at mom and she smiled approvingly.

"I think that would be fine Paul. Curfew is 11:00 though. I mean it. By 11:00 sharp, you will have returned Beth back here with us."

"Yes sir, that won't be a problem."

I walked Paul to his car. We hugged goodbye. He kissed me on the cheek and said,

"I would like to take you to a movie next Friday night. Would you like that?"

I felt so grown up. My first real date without chaperones.

"Yes."

"Great! Pick you up at 6?"

"Yes."

He was tall like my brother-in-law, Eric. They could even be brothers he looked so much like him with an accordion-cheeked smile.

I couldn't wait to call Lydia and tell her I was going on a real date! She was thrilled for me and shared her good news. She had just received a promotion, and Eric was getting noticed by more recruiters. The future was bright for both of them; and they would likely be moving to DC next year.

Mom and dad chatted with her too, and we all agreed to fly out there again to celebrate their second Christmas as husband and wife.

That following week we had what New Englanders call a cold snap. Although it was only mid-October, the frost was hitting overnight and as soon as the sun went down at about 4:30, there was a biting wind in the air.

That following Friday Paul showed up five minutes before 6:00 and helped me put on my warm wool dress coat. As he backed out of the driveway, the headlights of his parents' station wagon scanned across a swirling updraft of fall leaves. Reds, yellows and orange leaves danced in the headlights.

"Super windy tonight," Paul said.

"Yes, and cold too," I said.

On the 40-minute drive to the closest town

with a movie theater, we listened to music on the radio, and I started to hum along.

"You sing?"

"I did at my last school," I said.

"You should try out for choir. It's fun. We do a big Christmas concert every year."

"It's already October," I said.

"So, you should try. You have a really nice voice."

During the movie, he reached over and held my hand. I was beginning to like New Hampshire just a little bit.

After the movie, he drove me all the way to my parents' neighborhood but then he pulled into a street and stopped at a cul-de-sac where there was new construction. Bones of new house frames standing on bare cement foundations.

Why are we stopping?

"I brought a surprise for us," he smiled.

He got out of the car and went to the back of the station wagon and opened the trunk.

He sat back in the driver's seat holding a brown paper bag. He pulled two small paper cups and a bottle out of the bag.

"Do you like Cold Duck?"

"Cold duck?"

"Yeah, it's like a sweet champagne," he said, "it's really good."

"Alcohol?"

"Yes, look."

He reached up to turn the overhead light on

and held up the bottle to show me.

"I'm sorry, I don't drink."

"You don't drink? Have you ever tried?"

Should I tell him about my brother and the Budweiser last summer?

"I had champagne once for a toast at my sister's wedding."

"Don't you want to try it? It's really good."

He started to take the foil off the top of the bottle.

His tongue peeked out of his tight lips in concentrated eagerness.

When he popped the cork, I got a funny feeling on the back of my neck.

A familiar touch of fear like I felt around George.

"No thank you. I don't think I'd like it."

"Sure you will, c'mon, it's really sweet."

He poured some into a small paper cup that looked like the ones in the school cafeteria. Purple bubbles danced and crawled up the inside of the cup.

He drank it down in one swallow and poured some into the second cup for me.

"It's good," he said.

"I am too young to drink," I said, "I'm only 14."

He pressed off the overhead dome light and looked out the front windshield for what seemed a long time.

"Damn," he said, "I forgot about that."

With the bottle between his legs and the steering wheel, he slowly sipped the drink he had poured for me. Silently he sipped and stared out the windshield. His breath in the cold, fall moonlight.

How rude I am being, he planned this nice evening, we've had such a nice time, and now I have ruined it.

"I'm sorry," I said.

He finished what he poured for me, and clumped up the pieces of foil from the top of the bottle and pressed the plastic cork back in.

He nested the paper cups, put them on top of the corked bottle and into the bag.

He got out of the car and placed the bag in the back of the station wagon.

From the opened back door of the station wagon he said,

"I will take you home now," he said and slammed the trunk closed.

When we got to my house, he walked me to my door and leaned-in to kiss me.

"Sorry, I'm feeling pretty cold," I said.

"Me too," he said.

"Would you like to come in for a bit? I can make some cocoa for us. My mom has a really good recipe."

"I should go, it's late and I gotta drive at least another 40 minutes to get back to civilization."

"Thank you for a nice evening Paul, I really liked the movie."

"Yep. Goodnight. See you in class Monday!"

Monday before French class, he was waiting for me in the hallway outside the classroom.

"Hi," I said, thinking it was sweet that he waited to see me before class.

"Guess what I spent all day Saturday and Sunday doing?"

"I don't know, what did you do?"

"I spent the weekend cleaning the carpets of my mother's car."

What a nice boy to clean his mother's car after borrowing it. I smiled, but he looked angry, so then I was puzzled and said nothing.

"The Cold Duck. It *exploded* when it got below freezing on Friday night."

"Exploded?"

"Yeah, exploded," he said, his neck turning red, "I left it in the car thinking I would bring it to school for after the football game and it busted. The car stinks and my mom is furious! Except for band, I am officially grounded for a month."

"I'm sorry," I said, "that's sounds terrible."

"It's your fault," he said.

"What did I do?"

"If you had drank it like you were supposed to, it wouldn't have happened!"

"I don't -"

"I know, I know, you don't drink. You think you are better than us."

He started to walk away, then turned, pointed at me and said,

"And you know what? You're a cock tease that's

what."

He waved his spiral notebook at me as he walked backwards towards the classroom door,

"And you live all the way out in the boonies, who the hell will drive all the way out there to date you anyway?"

Deer in the headlights, I stood there and waited, debating if I should just skip class.

Where can I go? I can't go anywhere. I have to go to class; I can't bear to sit next to him. Not after that.

I imagined what Mom would say if I told her about it: *What did you do to make him say that?*

I paused at the threshold of class.

I wanted to disappear.

The teacher saw me and waved me in.

"Bonjour!"

I usually sat next to Paul in the front row, but I walked right to the back of the class instead.

I sat against the wall by the French magazines. Hemingway in his fisherman sweater smiled from the black and white cover of an old Paris Match magazine.

I had a great sense of relief when I remembered that our teacher had assigned us readings to translate, so we would be working individually that whole week.

Paul still chatting with Debbie looked totally different than he had with me just minutes before.

My body recognized that familiar feeling again

as I looked at his smiling profile and his animated gestures joking with Debbie.

It was the same feeling that I had in the car Friday night. That same feeling as when George asked me if I wanted to play fifty-two card pick-up.

He's so much like George. And mom wouldn't believe me if I told her what happened. "Your brother would never do such a thing. Don't you ever lie to me young lady."

I wasn't going to cry. I was determined not to.

I opened my notebook and started to write a letter to Joy:

Dear Joy, I hope you are doing well. I miss you guys so much! It's awful here. I am learning that school with boys is just horrid. Please tell Susan it's even worse than Mrs. Patterson's dance class we had years ago. The boys are SO distracting, and not only do they talk over you in class, but they also get called on more often. AND they interrupt all the time. AND worst of all, if they don't get what they want, they become total jerks.

DEATH AT 14

That dark Wednesday evening in late October, I heard my sister Lydia's voice unlike I had ever heard it before.

"Lydia, what's wrong?" I asked

"Please. Just put Mom on the phone."

Mom sensed something was not right because instead of her normal cheery greeting of, "Hello Dear, how are things?" she took the phone and said, "Lydia - what's wrong?"

I could hear my sister crying and her muffled words, "He's dead."

Mom steadied herself with her hand on the kitchen counter.

"OK," Mom said, "I'm putting your father on the phone."

She handed him the receiver. His blue eyes looked little boy scared, but his voice and body were all business.

He listened, then, "We will be on the first flight tomorrow."

When he hung up the phone, he took one breath, and reached for the thin yellow pages in the kitchen drawer.

Mid-dial, he hung up, turned to me and said,

"We'll have to have you stay with someone."

"Who will she stay with," mom asked, "we don't know anyone here yet."

There we were. The three of us.

New state, new home, new lives.

No friends.

Mom and dad had been quite social as soon as we'd arrived holding an open house before Labor Day and attending cocktail and dinner parties quite often. Leaving me alone most evenings while they connected with dad's network from his college and graduate school days.

And I, still so new at my school, I had not developed any real friendships yet either.

So there we were, me and my middle-aged stoic parents in stunned silence.

And then it was one of those moments where my whole body knew it before my brain registered how to say it. I blurted out in a tone of uncharacteristic defiance,

"She's my sister. And I'm going."

I walked upstairs to my bedroom, without waiting for their response or approval and started packing.

Hours before dawn, we were all in the car on our way to the airport.

When mom opened the bedroom door in their apartment the first thing I noticed was the smell.

The dog smelled it. He walked by the open bedroom door, black wet nose towards the room, then pulled his tail in tight to his rump, and scurried away.

The bed was just as the coroner had left it - blankets were bunched up on the right side of the bed where my sister usually slept. The top sheet was pulled back.

Stains.

There were stains on the white sheets. Remnants of Eric, brick red, brown and faint yellow. The brown was smeared as if the body was a brush on canvas.

I felt sick to my stomach. I swallowed and pointed to the sheets, "What's that," I asked.

Mom snapped on tight yellow kitchen gloves.

Snap. Snap.

She reached for his pillow and shook it from its case. Rust brown spots on the pillowcase. She threw the pillow on the floor, tossed the case on top of it.

"That pillow will have to be thrown out," Mom said.

She hated waste. She had been a depression era child who had to survive on two bowls of oatmeal a day, and wasted nothing, but even this could not be saved.

I walked towards the pillow to throw it out.

"Don't touch that," she said, "I'll do that."

She waved me back to the foot of the bed.

"Mom?" My voice quiet, as if I would wake someone.

"Yes?"

"What are those stains?"

Mom shook the other pillow out. Lydia's pillow. No stains. She wouldn't look at me.

"The body lets go after you die," she said, "grab that corner."

We pulled off the fitted sheet. Elastic corners snapped to the center.

"How could he die so young," I asked.

The stains had bled through to the mattress cover.

Mom pointed to the lower right corner of the bed.

"Pull that corner up over there."

I reached under the mattress, and peeled back the thick, tight elastic mattress cover.

"And how did she not know? The smell. I mean, she must have smelled it...right?"

With her yellow gloves, Mom folded the top sheet and bottom sheet in on themselves until the stain was hidden.

Then she pulled the four corners of the mattress cover up and around making a neat little bundle.

Stained cloth sagging with molecules of my 29

year old brother-in-law.

When she lifted the bundle of bedding off the bed, there was more. I swallowed down the sick feeling coming up from my stomach.

She paused and eyed the blue-striped mattress.

"We'll have to flip it," she said, and walked around the foot of the bed to the side where my sister usually slept.

Mom at the head, me at the foot, we lifted up the full-sized mattress on its side, then we pulled the opposite side out from under and it slapped down on the box spring.

"How could she not know he was dead before she kissed him?"

It was awful, and I could not understand it. My sister had been attending a two-day seminar for her new job and he had died in his sleep the one night she was away.

When she arrived home late that next evening to find the shades were drawn, the room was dark and she just leaned over to kiss him thinking he was asleep, but his lips were cold.

Mom walked over to the bundle of bedding and scooped it up in her arms. She walked out to the kitchen. I followed her.

She nodded towards the kitchen sink, "Get a garbage bag out. Please."

I opened the door under the sink, and pulled black plastic from the yellow box.

I shook open the plastic, and tried one more time, "And what about the dog - he was running around like crazy but refused to go in their bedroom. Mom, don't you think she knew something was wrong? Before, before she kissed him?"

I held open the garbage bag and she tipped her arms so that the fabric fell into the bag. Then she pushed the bedding down. Yellow gloves stuffing it in the black plastic bag.

She turned her head away. She snapped the rubber gloves off. Smell of sweat on powdery rubber on top of everything else, "Can't get blood stains out," she said, "now go wash your hands."

"Why is there blood?"

I stood there wanting mom to give me an answer. Anything to explain how such a thing could happen. How a young healthy man who ran several times a week would just die in his sleep.

Mom pulled the red plastic tape synching the bag up tight. Her fingers strained against the plastic ribbon tie wrapping the ribbon of red plastic around and around and around five or so times leaving just enough to tie a knot.

To make it air-tight.

To make sure nothing can come out.

She stood up straight.

Molecules of Eric wrapped in black plastic between our feet.

Finally, she looked at me directly, her brown eyes flat.

Her lips tight, "We will know more after the

autopsy. There's no point in speculating," she said, "now go wash your hands."

She held the bag away from her body and walked towards the front door. The dog followed her out onto the porch. Small Mom, wool-slacked Mom, walked outside with a bag that looked more than half her size.

Washing my hands in the kitchen sink I heard the metal trash can cover scrape open and the sound of plastic slipping against metal.

The bedding was gone, but the smell stuck in my nose. I went into the bedroom, pulled the blind cord, and opened the two small windows to let in some air. *How could she not smell it? How could she not know something was wrong?*

Dad left after he had been on the phone with Eric's family from Vancouver. They discussed funeral arrangements, and decided to have an autopsy since it was not normal for a healthy man of 29 to die in his sleep.

By late afternoon mom was still cleaning. The sliding shower door slammed back and forth, back and forth.

Crisp, leather shoes on tile, then on hardwood floor. Mom stood across the linoleum table from Lydia, holding a clear-handled toothbrush.

I knew that toothbrush, and I knew not to touch it. Just like the Michigan State sweatshirt hanging on the hook by the front door...not to be touched.

"I'm going to throw this out," mom said.

Lydia pushed her long black hair back from her face, stood up, and ripped the toothbrush out of mom's hand. She walked into the bathroom.

Mom followed her, and stood in the bathroom doorway, arms crossed in front of her.

If this were Mrs. Brady and Marcia, Mrs. Brady would hold her daughter and try to comfort her.

But my mom was not Mrs. Brady. My mom was bred from the harsh, winter light of strong, New England stock. She felt things very deeply, but had been taught to not show emotions to anyone except my father.

I walked over to the kitchen table.

The three of us now beads angled on a necklace.

My sister at the sink.

Mom, standing in the bathroom doorway.

And me, in the long shadow of Mom.

Lydia picked up the mug from the narrow glass shelf, placed Eric's toothbrush back inside next to hers, and sat the mug down without a sound.

Mom stretched her right leg back behind her. The dog started to pace behind her.

To be anyplace but here. Anyplace but in the middle of this thick, heavy sadness.

"Your father is meeting with the minister about the funeral. Do you want to go to the church and meet the minister?"

Church.

Mom believed that faith, prayer and a strong

work ethic could get you through anything.

At 14 I had a vague idea of faith at best, and a distaste for 'religion'.

✳ ✳ ✳

At the age of six I was kicked out of Sunday school for asking too many questions.

When the topic of "Father, Son, and Holy Spirit" came up I had asked,

"Why is Jesus with only his father in heaven?"

A low murmur and controlled giggles came from the boys sitting in the row next to me.

"Because that is what scripture tells us," she said.

"But where is the mother?"

"You just have to believe," she said, "and have faith in the Father, Son and Holy Spirit."

At my regular school, we were taught to ask questions if we don't understand, so I raised my hand again earnestly wanting the truth.

"But wouldn't Jesus' mom also be in heaven when she died?"

After a few more of my questions about Mary, it was clear I was confused, but the teacher could not answer me other than saying you have to have faith. But I had a mother and father, and if Jesus had a mother and father, why was he only in heaven with Father, and the Holy Spirit.

Then I asked the question that really got me in trouble,

"Is the Holy Spirit the ghost of Mary?"

In my mind it made sense, that way Jesus would be in heaven with both his parents, and that was all I was trying to understand.

Where was his mother?

The teacher's solution was to lock me in the coat closet for the remainder of the class. I whimpered in the dark, and tried to not gag on the sharp stench of mothballs.

When mom came to get me after church, they had let me out. I was a red-faced, scared and tear-stained mess.

I pointed to the coat closet and told her, "They put me in there."

"What did you do to make them do that?" Mom asked me.

The teacher approached my mother with perfect politeness and explained,

"I'm sorry but your daughter was being disruptive and I gave her a time-out. No harm done."

"I am so sorry," my mother apologized, "she has always been my most inquisitive child."

"How are Lydia and George? They were always such attentive and intelligent students"

The teacher looked down at me with a flash of contempt, "Very well-behaved."

"Thank you," mom responded while fixing my coat, "Lydia is spending a year on exchange in France and George was accepted at Yale, Dartmouth *and* Harvard!"

"I would expect nothing less," she said, "please

give them my best, I thoroughly enjoyed having them in class."

Mom fussed with my scarf and tied it a bit too snug.

"Perhaps this one is a late bloomer, maybe wait another year or two?"

They shook hands and then mom followed up with, "I am so sorry for your trouble, it won't happen again."

Mom squeezed my hand and pulled us towards the door. The same boys who had sat in the row next to me were standing around the doorway. They made faces at me and said,

"Cry baby... Such a guurrlll."

My mother in her crimson embarrassment did not hear it, or pretended not to.

"Do not tell your father what happened," she said as we walked fast down the corridor, "I will talk to him. And he will decide what to do."

My parents still insisted I go to church but instead of Sunday School classes, I sat with them in the pew for almost two hours. I noticed the people around me, frowning faces, fancy hats, lines of the oak grain, the frayed edges of the books, the texture of velvet. The organ music sounded so awful and depressing, but singing I liked.

When the grey old man would yell at us from a wooden box high up on the wall, I would look up, but did not understand anything he said. My neck hurt after service.

Mom and dad liked to go for cookies and coffee in the meeting hall after service, and now I went with them. It wasn't much better.

Almost every Sunday, the creepy minister in his long robes would make a point of coming over to speak with my parents.

He would pat my head and stroke my long hair and say, "What a pretty young lady you are." Or he would make a point of what I was wearing, "What a lovely dress you have on today. Very fine."

He was fat and smelled funny.

I began to dislike my long hair and my dresses.

I figured out how to time my request for a cookie until I saw him headed towards us. Once at the refreshment table, I would go slow and wait long enough for him to finish talking with my folks. He seemed to have caught on to this because he began to come over twice, and I was never allowed a second cookie, so then I would ask my father if I could get him a cookie. If dad said no, I made an effort to stand in-between my mother and father so that I would be harder for the minister's hands to reach.

He still tried.

That was the year I learned that my school was different than other classrooms, and asking too many questions or the wrong ones will get little girls locked in closets.

Or worse.

By fourteen I still believed in God in a general

sense, and the joys of Christmas in particular.

As for my exposure to death, my grandmother passed away when I was eleven. I was not allowed to attend her open-casket funeral, but mom asked me to help her clean out her house. It took us most of the summer.

Day after day we sorted the evidence of Grammy's life into either boxes for storage, or trash or public auction.

To mom's shock, I found several empty gin bottles in random places. They were tucked under her mattress, in the shoeboxes of her wardrobe, in the attic under the window, and in the drawers of my father's desk he used as a boy.

She had a house full of beautiful things: always fresh flowers in porcelain vases, small and large hand-painted clocks that chimed on the quarter hour in different tones, thick colorful oriental rugs under a beautiful Steinway grand piano, where she played Chopin for me. Delicate porcelain figurines kept her books company on the shelves, and the doors to her sunroom were held open by cast iron doorstops that were painted to look like sitting French Bulldogs.

Grammy's photos, travel journals and the deeply poetic love letters she received betrayed her stylish and poised demeanor.

My grandmother did not even have the right to vote, but she learned to play piano beautifully, studied Italian, French, Greek and Latin; read Jane Austen, George Elliot, Keats, Byron and

Wordsworth. She took photos of Byron's Bridge of Sighs in Venice with her very own Brownie snapshot camera, and sketched Bernini's Elephant in the Piazza della Minerva when she was in Rome.

She found the Roman Forum "too unbearably hot" to spend the day looking at "mostly dull piles of stone and random broken columns", but she fell in love with Botticelli's *Birth of Venus* in Florence and wrote that she found "painters to be much more interesting than poets."

Photos of her with her classmates on the streets of Rome and Paris - young women dressed in heavy Victorian clothing with large fancy hats and hands covered in gloves.

After her rare and privileged education, she returned to America to marry and settle into her role as wife and mother only to be widowed very young. Dad was only a teenager, and yet suddenly when his father died, he became the 'man of the house'. In later years she found comfort in her son's weekly visits, her grandchildren, and her increasing attachment to Gin Martinis.

Cocktails were introduced to society during her lifetime, and as a young bride she learned how to serve them at their elaborate parties, but after her husband died, grief was her constant companion, and it didn't matter whether she had company for cocktails or not.

At some point her comfort became addiction and what seemed fun and glamorous when she was young ultimately led to her painful death.

To me she was the much older grandmother who gave me wonderful Steiff stuffed animals at Christmas; served me root beer floats with vanilla ice cream in the summertime; and played Chopin for me on her piano while I daydreamed surrounded by beautiful things. It was the good the true and the beautiful to be in her home that was bright and airy full of light and color.

Hers was positive imprint that informed my love of creativity, classical art and beauty.

I would ride my bike to her house and sometimes she would come to our house to babysit me, but increasingly she would wear her sunglasses inside even at the dinner table.

During the last year of her life, she babysat me the night of a big thunderstorm that would be the last time mom and dad asked her to look after me. She sat in my desk chair in the middle of my bedroom. Frozen. The thunder became louder as the storm approached and the flashes of lightning lit up my bedroom windows with increasing frequency.

"Grammy what's wrong?"

"Stay away from the windows," she said.

She would not move. She just sat there in the center of my room in her navy wool dress, red silk scarf and dark sunglasses until the storm ended.

She didn't babysit me after that, and I was afraid of thunderstorms for years to come, but

I would still ride my bike over to visit her, and then, a few months later, she died.

A sad and tragic end that I did not understand at eleven, but I did grasp that death came to her when she was very old.

Grandparents grew old and older people were supposed to die, that was the nature of things, but not healthy young men who jogged several times a week and loved my sister.

Why did God allow such a vital young man in the prime of his life to die and cause such pain for those left behind?

And in his sleep.

That made it all even scarier because I had never heard of a young person dying in their sleep.

* * *

My sister closed her eyes. Her hands on porcelain, she leaned into the pedestal sink. I wanted her to rip the sink from the wall.

For someone to *do* something.

Anything, to show some emotion…some life.

I leaned into the robins-egg blue linoleum kitchen table and pressed my fingers hard into the aluminum edge.

I wanted metal to enter flesh.

Half-breaths make you invisible.

The apartment was cold. No insulation. My sister looked so small in her husband's robe. She was not the same woman who got married on my thirteenth birthday.

We will always remember the date. Now my birthday would be a reminder to her of not just their wedding day, but also his death, and this pain.

The five feet of white tile floor separating Mom and Lydia looked big, clean and shiny.

Lydia was wearing his brown wool socks. *Blood on sheets.*

Lydia took a breath bigger than herself, keeping her head down she pushed by Mom in the bathroom doorway.

"Leave the toothbrush alone. Just leave it Mother."

She sat down at the kitchen table behind me, pawing mindlessly through random envelopes. The bills she'd been paying cluttered the table.

"What is it you and Dad always say? Work will get you through?"

Mom walked over to the kitchen sink and picked up a sponge and turned on the water.

It seemed it was only a matter of minutes before Mom would suggest that the dog go for another walk. She would say something like,

"The dog looks like he needs to go out. It's so cruel to keep him locked up in here."

Or something like that, but never that mom needed air, or that it was cruel to keep us locked up in here.

In there.

Inside ourselves.

Alone. Together.

The wall heater made snapping sounds of metal expanding. My stomach nausea and cold hands. So many more feelings to ignore. Eight of my fingertips had deep indentations from the edge of the table. Imprints.

All of this an imprint.

Midnight. Lydia and I huddled under the thick, old quilts of the narrow guest bed. Her tears a slow wet through my nightgown. Her jaw moved against my shoulder and collarbone as she spoke,

"I was rushing to catch my plane to the conference that morning, and he wanted to make love."

My neck still bare in the dark chill of the room. She sucked her tears back in.

Her voice so quiet I could barely hear.

"I pushed him away. Told him there was no time."

She reached her hand across my waist. Her hand fidgeted with the sleeve of my flannel nightgown.

"He looked at me with those green-grey eyes, his hair all messy."

The sound of spit stuck on her tongue mixed with her words.

"Then he leaned over me, and whispered, 'C'mon, just a quickie.'"

Ever since her exchange year in France when she was seventeen, and I was only six, Lydia was very comfortable and open about the topic of sex. So comfortable to the point of having a heavy make-out session with her boyfriend on my bed that following summer when she was supposed to be babysitting me. She stopped when I walked-in on them only to laugh at my embarrassment and say, "Oh don't be such a prude!"

So comfortable as to explain in detail about how in France they "French kiss", and then there was the awkward time at Christmas one year when she questioned me about masturbation when I was too young to even know what the word meant.

But this, this was even more uncomfortable.

And then I felt guilty for feeling uncomfortable.

One tear lined my face cold down to the pillowcase. My throat hurt. I wanted to roll over and cry, but knew I had to be strong for her. She needed me to be the strong little sister, not the baby.

Her voice went away again, "I should have stayed," she said quietly, "How was I to know it was the last chance we'd ever have to be together?"

Pressing cloth.

She twisted the flannel of my sleeve tighter and tighter pinching my skin with it. Her body shook against mine with tears. I stroked her hair, trying to comfort her. Sadness mixed with guilt, salty tears and snot.

❉ ❉ ❉

The last time I saw Eric alive was their first and last Christmas as husband and wife.

Mom and dad and I had spent it with them, in this very apartment.

Christmas Eve, we went to a professor's party near campus. Tall Eric wore his forest green corduroy jacket with gray wool slacks. And those boots. Boots were the only shoes he owned besides his running sneakers.

A brilliant grad student with a promising future, he stood tall at the fireplace with his brandy on the mantle next to his right elbow, his left hand holding a spear in the fire. Roasting chestnuts and talking with two other students. Three spears roasting chestnuts in the fireplace.

Lydia and I sat on the couch a few feet away. He gave her that look.

That look that made me re-cross my legs.

He mouthed something to her about "getting her" later.

She laughed, turned to me and put her hand on my knee,

"Hey, is it OK if we break our tradition and don't sleep in the same bed this year?"

Her brown eyes - soft chestnut brown. In love eyes. In love eyes that went away forever after he died.

Lydia and I had this tradition to sleep in the same bed Christmas Eve, and Santa would deliver our stockings to the foot of the bed in the middle of the night.

We would spend the early pre-dawn hours opening our stockings together. Each item individually wrapped in green or red tissue paper and tied with thin ribbon. Even if it was obvious in its wrapping - like a toothbrush or the triangular shaped Toblerone chocolate, we'd giggle and ask each other "what could this be?"

After reaching the small canvas bag that held US Mint copper pennies in the toe of the stocking, we would carefully put each of the presents back into our stockings, and try to fall back to sleep until an acceptable hour.

But we never slept. We would catch up on school, her real boyfriends and my dreams of having one someday.

We talked and laughed, our faces inches apart on the pillows of my bed. Our stockings with crumpled red and green tissue and ribbons strewn around at the end of the bed like a Cubist painting.

That last Christmas, I became the jealous little sister,

"But we *always* do our stockings together, and we did it last year."

"Well Eric and I were not married yet last Christmas were we?" She said to me while smiling at him.

She rocked my knee back and forth, "We could open them together in the morning. It will be just like always."

"It's not the same," I said.

I hated myself for being such a brat. He was watching us. His forefinger tapped the chestnut at the end of the fire poker to see if it was done.

She looked over at him, "Eric?"

She moved her hand off my knee, and folded her hands in her lap.

Eric walked toward us with that big grin of his and floppy perfect hair.

"Yesssss," he said.

Lydia nervously smoothed her green Pendleton skirt over her knees.

"Getting our stockings together is kind of a tradition with us. Is it OK if you and I sleep apart just for tonight?"

His eyes over to me, then to back to her, "That's cool."

He smiled that big wide-jaw smile of his. His firm cheeks accordioned up behind the corners of his mouth.

Then he did that look, right *at* her. It was just a look, but so intimate it made my face hot.

"I'm sure we'll have plenty of Christmases together," he said.

❄ ❄ ❄

Now, in this same drafty apartment, in the same

guest bedroom where she and I had slept that Christmas eve, it had become the place where they would have no more Christmases.

Lydia's voice in low tones.

Then slow and clear she said, "Remember this: everything and everyone you ever love will be taken from you."

GIVING THANKS

After Eric's death, mom and dad became more involved in their church. Dad joined committees, and mom helped with every 'white elephant table' and charity event she could bake or knit for. It was a Norman-Rockwell-esque white steepled church nestled in trees and set back in time. Drafty, stark, and cold. The pews were painted white with thin cushions the cold seeped through.

The Sunday before Thanksgiving dad recruited me to help him deliver Thanksgiving turkeys to families in the area.

It was a bitter cold morning and we loaded twenty-five turkeys into the car after church service. These families received turkeys each Thanksgiving and Christmas from our church.

"Why don't you drop off this next one," dad

said as we turned onto Rattlesnake Road.

That same pot-holed road my school bus rattled down five days a week.

When dad turned into the driveway with the dented mailbox, I recoiled. It was Tommy's house.

"It's really simple," dad said, "you just walk the food up to the door, knock and they should be ready to receive it."

An old German Shepherd chained to the tree barked wildly; choking himself against his collar as dad pulled up the long driveway.

My hand on the door handle with a white-knuckle grip.

Do I have to?

With the engine running, dad got out of the Jeep Grand Wagoneer and opened the back. He handed me a large, covered, aluminum foil pan. It was big and heavy.

"I'll be right here," he said getting back in the driver's seat.

I walked up to the front door that looked more like an inside-house plywood door than an outside front door. Before I had to knock, the door opened wide and the man who I'd seen hit Tommy in the back of his head with a beer stood before me dressed just the same as he did the first day of school.

The noise and bright light of a large TV behind him and a recliner. Rust, shag carpet matted the floor.

"Hello," I said holding out the large aluminum container, "Happy Thanksgiving!"

His face was creased with ruts of graying stubble, and I tried to not look at the dirty stains on his protruding white t-shirt. The skin of his large stomach strained against the thin cotton.

When he took the container from me, his fingers grazed the back of my hand. His skin was rough.

His eyes darted over my shoulder to where dad was waiting, and then with his eyes back on mine, he took a step back and closed the door with his booted foot.

Hands in my jacket pockets I breathed deeply in and out through my nose a couple times fast hoping the cold air would erase the foul smell.

I walked back to my father waiting in the warm safety of our vehicle, and I wiped my nose with a fresh Kleenex from the glove box.

"How was it?" Dad asked.

"Gross," I said, "how can they live in that shack and yet have the biggest TV I have ever seen?"

The smell of the place still in my nose, I must have twisted my face in look of disgust. I could still feel the man's touch on the back of my hand.

"You are not to judge."

What?

"Dad he was rude; he did not even say thank you or anything."

"Look at me," he said.

I focused on the fancy script on the shiny

wood paneled glove box, *Jeep Grand Wagoneer*.

Dad grabbed my left elbow and squeezed.

"Look at me."

I turned towards him.

With his hand cupped around my elbow too tight, he pointed towards the house with his other hand.

"Do you think you are better than that man in there? *Better* than that family?"

I did. I did not see myself as that man who drank beer for breakfast. A man who beat his son and wore stained clothes and lived in a shack with no siding, but owned a huge TV.

Aren't I better than that man?

"Listen to me, you are not any better than him and shame on you for thinking you are. You were *born* into privilege, and you have a duty to give back. But you do not judge. You must never judge another person."

"I'm sorry, daddy," I said.

How awful I am. How selfish. I don't deserve what I have. Dad is right, who was I to judge this man? And yet, shouldn't I judge somehow the actions I saw that first day of school? This man who hit his own son on the back of the head?

I wanted to ask dad these questions, but he had both hands on the wheel now to turn us around and head back to the road.

"That is why I wanted you to do this with me today. You need to learn that not everyone has what you have."

I wondered if Tommy had been home. I wanted to turn around to see who might be watching us drive away.

Dad stopped again at the end of the driveway.

I closed my eyes, and listened carefully to my father's words:

"Remember this, Beth, you are no better than that family in there. You are privileged, but that does not make you any better than they are."

I felt terrible.

George's voice in my head again: *You little spoiled brat.*

Maybe Lydia and George are right, I'm still just a baby. A spoiled little baby.

The next day, Monday morning, Tommy walked up next to me between the bus and the school entrance.

Remembering what my dad had said the day before, I greeted Tommy as I would a friend,

"Hi Tommy, how are you?"

His strides timed with mine, he said in a low voice,

"We don't need your charity. You think you're better than us. Well, you're not any better than us, you rich, preppie, bitch."

He veered off and headed towards the smoking area. I walked up the steps to the building, my head spinning as I crossed the threshold.

What just happened?

Pitch, yaw and roll.

I didn't want to cry.

Something in me was different.

Tommy's words hurt, but the urge to cry wasn't there.

Instead, I heard dad's words from yesterday: *you are not any better than him and shame on you for thinking that you are. You do not judge. You must never judge another person.*

For Thanksgiving, mom and dad decided to fly back out to spend time with Lydia at the apartment. She was still living in the same place where Eric had died.

I was not allowed to go with them, but rather, after many conversations in hushed tones that I could not exactly hear, it was announced that I would be spending Thanksgiving with William Jr., Hope, Little Will and Benji.

I had not seen them since July and missed them all terribly.

Something wasn't right, but I was happy at the thought of spending time with Hope, and Little Will, so I kept my mouth shut, and didn't ask any questions.

Those few months since July, I was learning the art of ignoring what I don't want to know the answer to.

There was still no explanation for what I saw that day mom and I flipped the mattress. No explanation for why a twenty-nine-year-old man would die in his sleep.

It scared me to think about it.

And I thought about it.

Night after night, when mom and dad went out sometimes driving an hour away for a cocktail or dinner party and arriving home well after I had gone to bed, I would think about it.

Death.

There were no streetlights, and ours was one of only two houses on the entire street. The other house was a vacation home we had yet to see anyone enter.

No people for miles. I saw Stephan get on the bus every morning, but I had no desire to get to know him. He was stoned every morning, and he always looked miserable.

The next nearest family to me was likely Tommy's family on Rattlesnake Road.

Our new house was so tiny that the whole living room, dining room and kitchen would have fit in mom and dad's master bedroom in Providence.

The four TVs that were in different rooms of the house - gone.

Dad's three-thousand volume library from his den - gone.

The living room stereo, and extensive record collection - gone.

I loved music and always had the stereo on playing records or the radio. After my homework was done, and before dinner, I would turn on music and practice my floor routine for gymnastics in the living room to show daddy when he got home. Sometimes I would just sing along to hits on the radio using a spoon they gave away at the gas station as my pretend microphone.

Now in the New Hampshire house, the music of my old life had been replaced by darkness and silence.

Flying in thick clouds or fog, you can be pointing down and not even know it. Until it's too late.

Everything familiar was gone. Even most of my everyday objects and furniture I had grown up around.

Whenever dad or I asked about a specific thing we were looking for, like special holiday candle sticks, or a longed-for piece of furniture, mom would reply,

"The second-hand man got it."

My new bedroom was big enough for one dresser and my bed. The second-hand man got my desk, my desk chair and my bedroom chairs.

Dad's den furniture had also been downsized to fit in the 'loft' that overlooked the living room of our new house. There was only room for his desk, his desk chair and one of his leather armchairs with one small bookcase. Out of the three-thousand books that used to line the walls of his den in Providence, the only ones he kept were the set of Waverly Novels that he used to read as a young boy. I would not learn until a month before his death several years later just why those particular books were so precious to him.

I had been at the Cape when they packed

the house and mom informed me the day the moving van arrived in New Hampshire that my beloved desk and desk chair had gone to the second-hand man.

"We just have no room," she said. "This house is much smaller; we all have to make sacrifices. You can sit at my desk; we will put that in the guest room upstairs."

The small guest room next to mine had a twin bed in it from the summer house, mom's desk, and my tall bureau that was part of my bedroom set. The room was so small, even I had to walk sideways around the bed to get to her desk, and could barely pull the chair out to squeeze in and sit down. Mom made it clear that if I did use her desk, I was not to keep anything of mine in it. The tall bureau was off-limits too because she needed the extra room for her clothes which also filled the guest-room closet.

The few times I called Paul or Debbie from French class or my new friend Patty, mom made sure to tell me that it was a long-distance call, and it would incur a charge we couldn't afford.

"Make it quick," she would say, and then she would stand in the kitchen listening until I hung-up the phone.

Most nights when mom and dad dressed-up and went out to meet with their new friends, the only sound was Grammy's antique clock that chimed on the quarter hour.

One night, I turned on the clock radio in the

kitchen. One radio station came-in clearly and it played "golden oldies" from the 1950s. I didn't really like Elvis, so I turned it off and went up-stairs.

So painfully lonely and bored.

What little homework I had was done, and I had already written my letters to Joy, Susan and Maggie that week.

Almost on instinct, I pulled out an unused spiral notebook with an orange cover and MEAD stamped on it.

I have not written a personal journal since my very first one that I had in first grade.

* * *

The year I learned to write cursive in school, Grammy gave me my very first journal.

It was a small, gold vinyl diary with *My Diary* printed in gold script on the front with lined pages and a tiny lock that would click shut like a seat belt. The key was tiny, and I kept it in my desk drawer so I wouldn't lose it.

I would sit at my desk after I had finished my homework and write in my diary. I loved it. I would write even on Saturdays and Sundays too, especially if Paige had played at my house that week or if daddy and I had gone to the Athe-neum. It was the first time I wrote about my experiences, school, my hopes, the silly things Paige and I talked about, the games Little Will and I made up, and my observations of the world around me.

Lydia opened the little lock with a bobby pin and read it. She told me she read it, and then teased me about what I wrote one night when she was to look after me while mom and dad were out:

"Ha, ha, you want to drive a car like Speed Racer. Ha, ha, ha. He's a boy! Ha, ha! You are such a tomboy. You climb our dogwood tree and stare at the clouds? You think the birds sing for you? You and Little Will think you are spies and play that stupid game dinosaurs at Christmas time? That's just stupid - almost as stupid as you and Paige playing with your stuffed animals! You are such a baby."

She teased me for two days until I finally went to my room and locked the door. Crying, I took my diary from the bottom shelf of my bookshelf, where I had placed it next to my set of *Little House On The Prairie* books.

Not using the key, I tried to open it like Lydia said she had - with a bobby pin. I pulled the bobby pin that held my hair back from my face, bent it straight, turned it in the tiny hole, and the lock opened on my first try.

Stupid lock.

I read through all my pages, feeling naked knowing that Lydia's eyes had been there too.

She read my thoughts that were for me and my diary, not her!

With angry tears I separated the pages from the spine, and I tore all the pages in half and half again. I even scraped-off the gold "My Diary" from the cover using the edge of the bobby pin.

I carried the gutted cover, spine, and the torn pages in a pile all the way down to the boiler room in our basement.

Using my sweater, I turned the hot, open coil metal handle of that tiny door, and placed my pages into the flames.

Blinking my eyes from the intense heat, I watched them burn, not wanting a single scrap to be legible.

If I never write down my thoughts again, Lydia can't read them.

I watched as large chunks of ash danced into the updraft. I imagined the four stories they had to travel up through our cold, cavernous house to reach the sky.

Then I went upstairs, took the scissors from mom's bathroom, went back to my room, and cut my long hair off to look like Christopher Robin from *Winnie The Pooh*.

If Lydia was going to make fun of me for wanting to race cars like Speed Racer, call me a boy, and make fun of how Little Will and I played dinosaurs and spies; how I wrote about the clouds I saw when I sat in our dogwood tree in the yard, and how I liked to listen to the birds sing, and the animal kingdom games Paige and I made up, then I was going to make sure Lydia would never read my diary again.

I stood there in my red and white dress. The tear-stained little girl in the mirror with crooked bangs looked back at me crying.

My hair on the floor, on my shoes and dress. The ashes of my beloved first diary that Grammy had given me were somewhere in the sky.

I didn't get mad at Lydia who, like George, had been one of my caretakers since I was born. Instead, I took it out on myself. It was my fault. Even though there was no longer a diary for her to break into and read, by chopping my hair off, I unwittingly gave her one more thing to make fun of me with.

I was certain Mom would punish me and probably wouldn't believe me if I told her about Lydia reading my diary and what she said so I didn't tell mom.

Mom was upset that I had hacked my hair off, and I was not allowed to have Friday afternoon playdates for two whole weeks.

Mom said my hair would grow out, and she took me to her hairdresser the very next day to "make the best of the mess" I made of myself.

She never asked me why I cut it, and never mentioned it again once her hairdresser fixed it.

✳ ✳ ✳

Now at fourteen, I was going to journal again out of the desperate, painful loneliness I felt alone in our house in the woods, under the dark fall skies at the edge of the world.

I took my shoes off, crawled up on my bed and started to write holding my notebook in my lap.

What happens when we die? Why did Eric die so young? My sister loved him so much. Why did God let him die so young? Why do I have so much and yet Tommy's dad beats him and drinks a lot? Why couldn't I have stayed at my old school?

What if mom and dad get in a car accident and don't come home?

I wrote down every question that had stacked up in my head for months. Page after page my pencil raced along the lines of my spiral notebook, without me even thinking about it as if these questions had been buried deep and opened a flow of something old and new.

I had trouble seeing and realized that darkness had enveloped me.

It was now 10:30 PM, and I had written fifteen pages front and back.

An odd feeling of being outside of time and outside of myself. The questions, sentences and paragraphs pushed themselves through my pencil and onto the page.

I no longer felt quite so alone, and then I wrote almost automatically,

It's the first time you've really thought about me since I died.

I closed my notebook and asked the empty room,

"Eric, why did you have to die?"

I had a headache from writing all that time in only the dim light of the hall lamp coming through my open door. I set my notebook carefully on my bureau, and placed my pencil with its lead worked down to a dull point on top of it. I opened the drawer of my bureau and took out my beloved fountain pen. I thought of my sister and how I'd wanted to have ink-stained fingers like she did. I thought about my first diary, and how she broke into it, and read it.

I felt in my body that the writing I had just done freed me, relaxed my mind, and brought me comfort.

Then I thought about last Christmas and how I insisted Lydia keep to our Christmas Eve tradition, and how it was their first and last Christmas Eve as husband and wife.

I was so selfish.

I'm such a baby.

I put my hand to my face and realized it was wet. I had been crying, seeping.

I can't think about this now.

I put my fountain pen back in the drawer. I felt hollowed out. I had not cried since dad held me on the steps of the chapel.

* * *

The day of Eric's funeral, I was fine until we walked out the steps of the small university chapel and I saw a long line of black limousines glinting in the crisp fall sunlight.

Doors.

I seemed to always fall apart when walking through doorways. Stepping over thresholds.

I fell apart, just like on the steps at William and Hope's house at the Cape that perfect July day when mom told me on the phone we were moving.

I had no control over my body, and it heaved. Through my blurred vision, this time it was not Hope, but my father walking towards me. He hugged me, gave me his handkerchief and I cried as he walked me to the car.

❈ ❈ ❈

Alone in the purple-black darkness and silence of a desolate New Hampshire autumn night. In our new house on that dark, empty cold street - I was alone at what seemed to be the edge of the world.

I washed my face and hands turned the lights on and went downstairs.

I turned on every light downstairs too as if by electricity I could push away the darkness. I knew I would have to turn them all off again except for the front porch light because dad always said to turn them off if you are not using them. Between the phone and the lights, it was as if mom and dad were back in the depression era frugality of their childhood.

Conserve electricity and don't make phone calls, but dad bought a very expensive car? It makes no sense.

Even though I felt more relaxed from writing everything down, the fear came back so easily.

If I have the lights on, I feel less alone, but we have no curtains, so if there is someone out there, some scary person in the woods, they could see me clear as day.

I turned off the kitchen light, leaned over the counter towards the window, cupped my hands against it and tried to see our back yard.

Total Darkness.

I miss my friends and school so much.

No moonlight?

Not even a single star.

The outside matched my insides.

I opened the kitchen cabinet where dad kept his bottles. At the end of every day, he still made his cocktail just like when he worked at the bank. He always whistled when he mixed his gin and tonic and was even more cheerful when they had guests and he had reason to make fancy drinks like martinis using the shaker.

There was not one day in my life so far when I did not see dad have a cocktail before dinner.

I thought of how sick my brother's dare to drink his beer and backwash made me that summer, and I was glad I did not accept Paul's offer of the Cold Duck.

It tastes so awful, why do people like it so much?

There must be something to it.

I was curious that night, but not curious enough to do anything about it.

I closed the kitchen cupboard and opened the fridge.

I poured a glass of milk, drank it over the kitchen sink, rinsed my glass and put it in the dishwasher. I turned off the downstairs lights and went back upstairs to my room.

I opened my suitcase and put my orange, spiral notebook underneath my clothes.

Lydia was not even in the same state, but I now had the learned reflex to hide my writing. I tied the two ribbons that held my folded clothes in place in my suitcase and went to bed.

On Wednesday, my brother William Jr. arrived to drive me to Connecticut for Thanksgiving.

After a quick bite, we were in his boxy Volvo, and backed out of the driveway.

Once on the main road, he took the bottle of Pepto from behind the stick shift and gulped some from the bottle.

"Are you sick," I asked.

"Nope," he said, wiping his mouth with the back of his hand, "I'm fine."

Keeping his eyes on the road, he handed me the bottle and the cap, "Here," he said, "put this back on for me."

I put the cap on and wedged the bottle back in the space behind the stick shift.

I liked riding in his Volvo. The front passenger seat hugged me.

William Jr. drove fast, but I always felt safe with him. He didn't tailgate the cars in front of him like dad did, but he drove much, much faster.

He kept his eyes on the road and checked his mirrors with a rhythmic frequency.

Rear view, left, right, rear view, forward.

Repeat.

After a couple hours on the road, we finally stopped at a Howard Johnson's. I needed to use the restroom and he decided we should both get a little something to eat. I ordered a vanilla milkshake, and he got a hot coffee with toast.

"How do you like New Hampshire?"

"It's alright," I said, "I miss my friends and school horribly."

"Really weird about Eric, huh? Damn, what crap luck Lydia has always had," he said to his coffee cup.

It seemed like he was referring to something specific.

"Crap luck?" I asked.

"Well, yeah, first her best friend, Gracie, dies at thirteen right in front of her when they are horseback riding together, and then in upper school, that girl in her class was murdered."

"What??"

I had not known of any of these things.

"What are you talking about? Mom said Lydia

stopped riding because she broke her back."

"Yes, that's true, she broke her back when *both* horses spooked. She was not riding alone that day. Lydia got lucky, but Gracie landed her skull on a rock, and the horse landed on her. Gracie died instantly, right in front of Lydia who couldn't even move to try to help."

I looked at my milkshake.

"That's horrible! Why did Lydia never tell me?"

"You were too young," he said.

"I'm always too young," I said.

The waitress came by and refilled his black coffee.

William Jr. added three heaping teaspoons of sugar.

I waited.

I wanted to ask but was too scared of the answer.

After stirring his coffee for what seemed forever, he set the spoon down on the table and said,

"And the *other* is why she went to school in France for a year. Mom and dad thought it best to get her away from it all during the murder investigation. Lydia had been with her that night, and it happened just after she left. She was a mess. A total mess."

"It happened at her friend's house? Who was she?"

"Yes, it was the ... well I shouldn't tell you, but you used to walk by the house every day on your way to school. They had been best friends ever since Gracie died."

William Jr., frowned as he looked out the window at the parking lot, then said,

"It was like she took the place of Gracie for Lydia. And then she died too. And now Eric has died on her. Crap luck."

I shivered a chill through my body.

Everything and everyone you ever love will be taken from you.

"Look, I shouldn't even be telling you this. It's best you don't know some things. Mom and Dad are trying to protect you."

"Did they ever catch the guy?"

"No. I don't know... I don't think so."

He looked out the window,

"As far as I know, when she got back from France, it was never mentioned again. And I was married, so I had Hope and Little Will to worry about."

He re-positioned his coffee cup in the saucer and wiped his mouth with a napkin.

He looked me in the eye, like he was going to say something else. He crumpled his napkin, looked at my milkshake and said,

"You almost done there? We should get going."

He smiled. He like my mother, had mastered the art of changing the subject. I was still learning.

At least he is not mean to me like George is. And he just told me a huge family secret that no one else had.

I wondered how many other secrets had been kept from me.

I sucked down the last of my yummy vanilla milkshake all the way to the bottom and made the empty-straw sounds.

"You use the ladies' room again if you need to while I go pay, and I'll meet you in the car."

Back on the road I fell asleep only to wake when we pulled into the driveway safely in Connecticut.

It was late and it was dark.

The light of their back porch haloed Hope's body as she walked out to greet us.

Seeing Hope I was no longer tired; I no longer felt scared or alone.

It was as if seeing her put a burst of sunlight in my chest directly.

She kissed William Jr. as he stretched the hours of sitting out of his body, and then he enveloped her in a warm, but short, hug.

"Hi Beth," she said.

I wanted to run to her.

To knock her down with my hug like an untrained puppy.

Does that make me a baby?

"Hi," I said.

To my brother she said,

"The boys finally got to sleep," then she turned to me, and we all walked towards the trunk of the car.

"They are so excited to see you, but we have

to be quiet and not wake them, or they will be cranky monsters tomorrow."

William Jr. pulled my suitcase out from the trunk and set it down in front of me. He closed the trunk without making a sound.

"Alright," he whispered, "let's get inside."

WHITMAN &
GINSBERG

Mr. McG assigned us *Leaves Of Grass* by
Walt Whitman because Mr. McG said
Whitman was the "Literary Father" of
Allen Ginsberg who wrote *Howl*.

On that fateful day, in December 1979, James
Allan asked, "Is he kwee-ah?"

"What's that James?"

James Allen squirmed in his chair, and pointing to a page in the poem, he said,

"He's talking about men and boys as if he..."
James Allen could not finish his thought.

Mr. McG's voice softened and said, "It's alright,
James, go on."

The class got real quiet.

James Allen's girlfriend looked over at him and his face turned red.

Mr. McG smiled, "Are you asking if he was of the Oscar Wilde persuasion?"

Heads turned to see if anyone knew what he was referring to.

Oscar Wilde Persuasion?

Mr. McG put his open copy of *Leaves of Grass* down on his desk and walked up to the chalk board.

He picked up the chalk and wrote out in huge, printed letters: "HOMOSEXUAL".

His back to us, chalk still in his left hand, he rolled up his sleeves.

I stared at the letters.

I had never seen it in print, but I had heard that word before.

One time when I was hiding in the sunroom I overhead my mother talking to my father.

It was one of those times I heard something I wasn't supposed to hear.

"Homosexual."

＊ ＊ ＊

It was a word that I had heard my mother use with other words like: "Deviant" and "Anita Bryant" and "Bathhouse".

Words that accompanied my mother's expression that I glimpsed through the crack in the door. And my father's prolonged silence. Hiding in the sunroom that day when I was small enough to fit behind the sunroom door under the nested end tables next to the couch. To listen and peek undetected. I did not know what they were talking about but I remembered those words, and the glimpse I caught of my mother's face as she said them. The look on her face scared me.

❋ ❋ ❋

Mr. McG turned to face the class slowly. He raised his head to look at all of us and said in his big voice,

"Oscar Wilde, was a homosexual."

He turned back to the board and underlined the word.

Mr. McG turned toward us and said,

"Walt Whitman, was a homosexual."

He underlined the word again, then turned toward us.

"Allen Ginsberg, my dear friend, *is* a homosexual."

He turned back to the board, and underlined it a third time and fourth time.

He put the chalk down and briskly slapped the chalk off his hands.

We all sat there stunned.

Looking at each other mouths opened.

His back to us.

What is happening?

James Allen's copy of *Leaves Of Grass* fell off his

desk and slapped down on the tile floor.

Then after what seemed an eternity, Mr. McG turned to face us again. He took a deep breath, smiled and said slowly,

"And I. I too am a homosexual."

The bell rang.

Everyone made for the door in a scramble of legs and arms.

Except for me.

Except for James Allen.

I was still thinking about my mother, remembering how her face looked through the crack in the door and my father's silence.

Mr. McG picked up James Allen's copy of *Leaves of Grass* off the floor, closed it, and set it on James' desk.

I got up and walked quietly towards the door. Then in a soft tone of voice I had never heard out of Mr. McG before, he said to James the words he had said to me on the first day of school,

"Remember, kid, you're tougher than you realize."

The following week, Mr. McG was gone, and we had a substitute teacher.

The Monday after that, it was announced in homeroom that James Allen committed suicide.

LONDON BOY

The house next door and the only other building on the street was a vacation home, and mom noticed there was a car in the driveway. Finally, after almost a year, there were other people on our street!

In mom's proper form she brought over a fresh plate of cookies to welcome them, and she returned with a full report.

Dad and I were reading on opposite ends of the L-shaped couch that dominated our tiny living room.

"Our neighbors are from London," she announced.

"A lovely couple, David and Judy Pemberton. He's in banking and she's a classically trained musician. Now in retirement she's become a painter."

Mom's energy was spilling over.

She sat down on her rocking chair forming a perfect triangle with me and dad.

"William, they invited us to have dinner with them tonight," she said to Dad who had to be persuaded to put down his WWII history book.

"That's fine," he said, "I have a nice bottle of scotch I can bring."

Mom turned to me, her face bright with excitement,

"Beth, you are invited too. They have a son about your age, he attends boarding school in Scotland, and they are all here for the next six weeks."

Although mom and dad had made friends from dad's college connections and their church, it was revelatory for all of us to finally have other humans in our neighborhood.

Mom was lonely too, maybe even more than I was, but neither one of us talked about it.

The day we moved-in last summer, I had become visibly upset about the move and cried in front of them. Dad had scolded me, *Be grateful! You have a roof over your head and food on the table!*

When dad suddenly decided to move for a reason not yet explained, he had not only pulled me out of school, but also took mom away from an administrative job that she loved at an art college in Providence. And he took us both out of a house we loved.

I didn't know it then, but mom was just as lonely as I had been that year. And although we had gone to church and even spoke privately as a family with the minister after Eric's death, they were still stoic and our communication as a family didn't get any better.

Mom looked at me, her face one of hope and happiness that I had not seen since Lydia's wedding.

"Maybe their son is someone you can play tennis with this summer, dear, or perhaps go sailing together."

Sunfish boats and Blue Jays were allowed on the lake and could be rented by the hour. It was a modest lake, a key feature of the new community that was building homes and attracting vacationers during the summer.

Later that evening, the three of us walked down our driveway and turned to walk up their long white gravel driveway. The tall birch and pine trees between our houses created a row of white and green leading the way to their house that was set farther back from the road than ours. Walking up the long gravel driveway I could see it was at least three times ours. Boxy and modern, with gray stained siding and lots of windows on the second floor. No porch, just three modest wooden steps leading up to a large red door.

"Go ahead," mom encouraged.

I walked up the steps first. The front door had a large, brass lion's head knocker on it.

Reaching for the knocker, I could feel the tightness of my dress across my chest and shoulders. Mom insisted I dress-up for dinner, but all I had was my 8th grade summer dress that now, a year later, was too small across my chest and shoulders. Mom gave me a cardigan to hide that it didn't fit me right, and now I was too warm.

I brought the knocker down on the lion's head three times.

Mr. Pemberton opened the door.

"Welcome," he said, "you must be the lovely Beth."

His London accent was music to me. I had never heard one before. As I shook his hand, my body wanted to curtsey, but instead I looked him in the eye and said,

"Nice to meet you Mr. Pemberton."

"Oh please, call me David, that's just fine," he said.

Judy, his wife, walked up behind him wiping her hands on a dishtowel and then lifting them overhead, she waved us in.

"Greetings, welcome, welcome."

She had stylish black hair with gray highlights, cheerful smiling eyes and wore a modest, fashionable dress with heels. She and mom had similar taste in clothes.

Their house was deceptively simple and plain on the outside. But once inside, it opened up to cathedral ceilings and exposed wood beams with floor-to-ceiling windows facing an enclosed yard.

It was not just another house; it was another world. A gorgeous mix of classical and modern. Geometric flat, gray-stained siding on the outside, with warm wood tones, vibrant colors and rich textures on the inside. They were only there a couple months a year and yet it felt like more of a home than ours did.

Polished rough-hewn uneven barn plank flooring was accented by thick, colorful wool rugs placed throughout and a baby grand piano that reminded me of Grammy's Steinway.

A beautiful chrome and cherry wood stereo system nestled between two built-in, floor-to-ceiling bookcases that covered the west wall. They even had one of those rolling ladders to reach the upper shelves like the one at the Providence Atheneum.

A record floated on the turntable, and the delicate sound filled the room so finely as if to put us in a concert hall.

Drawn to the wall of books and soothing piano music, I forgot my manners and walked directly towards the stereo.

Mom followed me, and over my shoulder she said quietly,

"Beth, do you like this music?"

"Yes," I said.

I felt this music. I knew this music deep in my

bones. A sense of comfort came with it that I could not explain.

She placed her hand gently on my shoulder and continued,

"I used to listen to this every day when I was pregnant with you. It's Chopin's Nocturnes. Over and over again as I rocked in my rocking chair. I was so happy to be pregnant with you."

"I love it," I said.

My body knew that music, that love.

I turned to look at her and saw in her eyes the love I had so longed for her to show me.

I wanted to hug her like I hugged Hope.

But she had already turned away from me with the words,

"Judy, what can I do to help?"

She walked to the kitchen, and it was over.

The books and turntable behind me, I watched my father hand Mr. Pemberton his prized bottle of scotch.

The tradition between men of that generation always involved a good bottle of scotch. My dad revered it so.

Mr. Pemberton was about the same age as my dad and standing near each other, they could be brothers, both with gray hair, a modest pot belly, tweed jackets with suede patches on the elbows and nice slacks. My father wore his yacht club tie and Mr. Pemberton, I mean David, wore what looked to be a school tie or a family crest that I could not make out from a distance.

Judy led us over to the living room seating area. Mr. Pemberton made cocktails, and then dad and Mr. Pemberton sat in the plump chocolate brown leather armchairs facing each other. Two matching leather couches also faced each other forming a loose rectangle around a beautiful mahogany coffee table.

I recognized the coasters as the same ones mom had at the 'white elephant table' from church and realized she must have brought them as a housewarming gift.

The chestnut brown couches were draped with colorful angora blankets and creme damask pillows. Everything was so inviting and lovely.

I sat down on the couch closest to the bookshelves, and mom and Judy brought out two plates with cheese and crackers.

Mom handed me a glass of club soda, and I took a coaster from the stack in the center of the coffee table, and carefully sat my glass down.

Mom and Judy sat on the couch opposite me.

Judy glanced up and said,

"Oh, lovely, here comes our son. Toby, our dinner guests are here, come say hello!"

"Yes mum," he said.

His words floated-in on the notes of Chopin and I turned around to see a blond boy who looked familiar. He wore a pink oxford shirt and a tie that looked the same as the one his dad was wearing. Toby's khaki pants were rolled up one turn at the bottom.

"Son, put some shoes on. We are not at the beach."

"Yes father," he said, and spun right around on his heels, and bounded back up the stairs two at a time.

Judy smiling said, "that's our son, Toby."

Shaking her head she continued, "He just loves this modern American idea of walking around barefoot all the time."

Toby came back down a minute later.

"That's better," Mr. Pemberton nodded in approval. Toby approached my parents with his hand outstretched in a polite greeting.

Mom, dad and I stood up to meet him.

He looked familiar to me like the Ralph Lauren models I had seen in the pages of the Sunday New York Times Magazine.

I reached out my hand to meet his.

"Nice to meet you, Toby," I said, "I'm Beth."

"Brilliant," he said smiling.

"You're the girl who made my ice cream cone the other day!"

That's where I'd seen him.

I had been so stressed about scooping ice cream and running the cash register with the line of people clamoring for ice cream, I had barely looked at him that day.

"Nice to meet you," I said, "I hope your ice cream was alright."

"Yes," he said, still shaking my hand and looking directly into my eyes.

His hand was strong and smooth. One moment too long, and we both got shy. He put his hands in his pockets.

He had on Top Siders.

With no socks.

Like me.

Like George.

"So, you two have met," Mrs. Pemberton said.

"Beth works at the ice cream stand down by the lake," mom said, "her first *real* job."

My first real job was the one mom insisted wasn't a job, and yet at the same time the one she claimed Hope paid me too much for. That was last summer, when I was a nanny for Hope and the kids at the Cape. I knew not to argue the point, and it would be rude to even mention it in such polite company.

"I just started this week," I said to Mrs. Pemberton, and then to Toby, "You met me on my first day, I was a bit nervous."

"You did great," he said, "best chocolate chip cone I've ever had."

Dinner was delicious. Grilled salmon cooked to perfection. Served with a garden salad of red and green lettuce, cucumbers, sunflower seeds, tomatoes and tiny cubes of raw yellow squash. The dressing was a honey vinaigrette that was tart and sweet on my tongue. For dessert Judy served a lovely strawberry shortcake with homemade fresh creme that mom helped her whip up in the blender.

"These strawberries are from the local farm stand," Judy said, "it's just lovely all the fresh vegetables and fruit you have here during the summer. "

Toby laughed and said, "Mum thinks she will start a garden someday, but she doesn't have a green thumb at all."

"Phhttt," she said to her son tapping his hand and they both laughed.

I was taken aback by the way Toby addressed his mother; his casual jest reminded me of Hope's conviviality.

"Well, it's true," he said, "she's a wonderful mother, brilliant painter and classical pianist, but when it comes to planting...we have a gardener."

"My grandmother played piano beautifully," I said, "Judy, would you please play the piano for us after dinner?"

"Beth, that's rude," mom scolded, "we are their guest."

"I'm sorry," I said feeling embarrassed.

Judy smiled and said, "Beth, it would be my pleasure. Perhaps during after-dinner brandy, I can play a little something."

Mom talked about our garden up on the hill and offered to show Judy, and then the usual topics of school and colleges, politics and business were discussed. It reminded me of the wonderful dinner parties mom hosted back in Providence. I couldn't wait to tell Joy that we finally had neighbors!

After dinner, Mr. Pemberton poured us all a brandy. He handed one to Toby who was my age and then asked my father if I would have one too.

"Yes, but please pour her just a small taste," dad said to Mr. Pemberton.

I felt so grown-up when Mr. Pemberton handed me the beautiful crystal brandy glass with amber liquid that caught the light.

Judy sat down at the piano, Toby on the couch, mom and dad were in the leather chairs and Mr. Pemberton sat at the end of the other couch, with his body turned so he could see his wife at the piano.

"Beth, I noticed how much you appreciated Chopin's Nocturnes," Judy said, "shall I play something else by him?"

"That would be wonderful, thank you," I said.

"Alright, this is known as his Ballade number 3 in A flat major. He composed it at Nohant, France when he was deeply in love."

The music brought images of blissful summer afternoons in Grammy's sun-drenched living room surrounded by beauty when she'd make me a root beer float with vanilla ice cream and then play piano and talk about her life.

That was years ago, when I was just a child, but I still missed Grammy so much.

And now, Eric was gone.

And Mr. McG, the only teacher I liked at my new school, was gone.

And James Allen was gone in such a tragic way that I could not even talk about it with mom or dad.

My friendship with Joy, Susan and Maggie lived-on in letters but they were becoming less frequent.

And here is this heartbreakingly handsome smart boy sitting next to me with parents who are affectionate, jovial and warm.

A wall of books filled with literature like dad's old den behind me.

Judy's lovely paintings on the wall next to other paintings I didn't know, but found equally beautiful like the Italian paintings on the walls of Grammy's living room.

I was becoming a woman and in that moment the music, the beauty of life and death, love and loss, loneliness and isolation transfigured.

The brandy burned my nostrils at first, but then became as warm and delicious as the notes Judy played.

My dad, Mr. Pemberton and Toby holding their snifters of brandy, mom on the edge of her chair leaning forward in rapt attention. The horrible, lonely winter I'd survived alone in the silence of our house. All the sadness, the whole year of death, change and loss. I felt a glimmer of happiness push against the darkness and break through. I looked over at Toby and he smiled a kind smile at me.

All the beauty of that moment: the sweet, strong taste of the brandy, the pain of time past and the brightness of hope rolled into the notes of Chopin's Ballade No. 3 Opus 47 in A flat major and took root next to his Nocturnes in the deepest chambers of my heart.

After Judy finished playing for us, we gave her a standing ovation and she stood to bow.

There was a silver framed black and white photograph on the wall behind her that I had noticed while she was playing. She caught my eyes looking at it.

"That's a family portrait we took last Christmas," she said walking behind the piano bench, "we get one done every year."

There were four people in the portrait, Mr. and Mrs. Pemberton, Toby and a girl with long hair that looked similar to Toby but older. They were all smiling like they all knew the same Something, and it was good and rich, and even funny. Real smiles always change the eyes.

Mom walked over to join us and take a look.

"That's our oldest child, Lily," she said.

"She's beautiful," mom said.

Hearing those words come out of mom's mouth, I realized, were words she'd never said to me.

"She's alright," Toby said with a joking tone standing behind us.

"Hopefully you will meet her either this Christmas or next summer," Mr. Pemberton said, "She's on her gap year right now on a "Grand Tour" through Europe.

"Grand tour," I asked, "with a tour group?"

Toby laughed, "The Grand Tour, it's what we do before going to Uni. Just like Goethe, Stendhal, Keats and Byron and many others. It's tradition."

"That's what Grammy did when she was young," dad said, "Remember her pictures and her journal you found?"

"Yes," I said, "Of course." Feeling embarrassed.

How could I forget her journal? I loved it so.

Dad continued, "The pictures she took in Venice and Rome were when she was trying to find the locations Byron described in *Childe Harold's Pilgrimage*."

"That sounds lovely," Judy said.

"Brilliant," Toby said, "when I go I want to see Rome the way Stendhal did. What year did she go?"

"She went in 1910, and traveled for a year" dad said, "with a group of other American girls on the Lusitania, actually."

"That's amazing," Toby said.

"Quite lucky she wasn't on the Lusitania in 1915," Mr. Pemberton said, "or we wouldn't be sitting here having this conversation!"

"Ah, the mysteries of life," Judy said, "Isn't it grand? Our dear Lily was accepted at Brown and Cambridge," Judy smiled, "we are hoping she will make up her mind somewhere between Naples and Greece and inform us of exactly where she wants to go."

Mom sat up straighter and said, "I went to Brown. Well it was Pembroke for the women when I attended."

"Oh, yes," Judy said, "just like Radcliffe was for the women who went to Harvard."

"Yes," mom said, "I am hoping Beth will attend Brown, but that remains to be seen."

I thought of Joy, Susan and Maggie. For most all of my former classmates it would be a decision of *which* Ivy League school to attend, but where I was now, the question for most was *if* they would even apply to college.

"What happened to Grammy's journal," I asked, "I'd love to look through it again, and show Toby."

Mom looked over at dad.

"We must have it somewhere," dad said, "surely the second-hand man didn't get that."

The air became tense and Mr. Pemberton graciously changed the subject and said,

"Toby wants to look at Dartmouth while we are here this summer, perhaps you would like to join us, Beth?"

"I would love to," I said, "I have to work tomorrow, but I have Thursday and Friday off."

"Perfect, we can make a day of it," Mr. Pemberton said.

My father was thrilled, and so was I. Toby

was so smart. He was well-read like George, but funny and warm like Hope.

At dinner the way he held his fork and knife reminded me of George, he too had started doing that after he went to boarding school. He had perfectly trimmed nails that reminded me of George's. I got a funny feeling when I looked too long.

When we got home, I wanted to ask about Grammy's journal. I so hoped it was somewhere in the boxes of dad's closet, but was not going to ask.

Thursday morning, I answered the door to a grinning Toby.

"My father is on his way up," he said, "I thought I would be the first to greet you."

His enthusiasm was contagious.

Toby had not a care in the world, and he made me feel that way too.

I looked out and saw his father walking up the driveway, he waved, "Good morning!"

Mom had prepared pecan sticky buns which were my favorite, but she forbids me to have one.

"Sugar is bad for your waistline, young lady," she had said to me when I tried to taste one earlier, "and you have such lovely teeth, you don't want cavities."

Mom was convinced I was getting fat and she insisted after my 15th birthday that I eat what she eats every morning.

"Grapefruit burns fat" she'd say, and "it's important to always start your day with breakfast." My body was becoming more and more that of a woman, but to mom, my no longer fitting in 7th and 8th grade clothes was what she called "getting fat."

David and Toby greeted my father with enthusiasm, and I found myself looking forward to spending the day in the company of three gentlemen. I didn't mind having toast and grapefruit. Toby's smile and good attitude washed away any negativity in the room.

Toby and I sat in the backseat of dad's Jeep Grand Wagoneer. It was a long drive, and I was grateful for the comfortable seats and fine interior. Somehow the fact that Toby was sitting next to me gave me more appreciation for dad's choice of vehicle.

We toured the campus and then Dad took us into Baker Library. It was beautiful.

"Daddy, it's like the atheneum," I said. The walls of books were set in oak floor-to-ceiling shelving with ornate iron grates on the second floor aisles that overlooked the main seating area. Green leather reading chairs faced large windows in between stacks of books.

When we moved, mom literally threw away so much. My father had a library of over 3,000 volumes. The library where I went to pull Nancy Drew and The Hardy Boys books off the shelf was just a painful memory.

Why did my parents dump everything and move us to a tiny house in the woods with no books, no stereo and no TV?

The painful longing came up in me. My desire for things to be as they had been. My desire to be at my old school where I was engaged, growing and learning. Gymnastics and art. My new school did not even offer art or gymnastics. I got good grades without even trying. It was so different than my other school, the classes were so boring. Mr. McG was the only teacher who was interesting and he made me think, and now he had left suddenly and no one would even mention his name.

I did homework and the assignments, but I wasn't challenged at all, and I had learned to not ask questions or answer them too often because the other students didn't like it. Especially when a girl looked smarter than a boy in class. I slowly became one of them, indolent, rolling my eyes when this one student raised her hand again. She was a know-it-all and not very nice.

So how to be a good student, and love learning like I used to, and find friends like Joy, Susan and Maggie? I want to learn, and I don't want to be ridiculed for it. Patty is pretty nice, but we don't talk about books and French classes like Joy and I used to. It seems the only thing people here at my new school like to talk about is boys, and parties, who is dating who, football and what was on TV the night before.

I wasn't really aware of all the psychological

changes that were happening. Just that I was painfully lonely, felt more stupid and seemed to be less of a person than I was one year ago.

"You ok," Toby asked.

He had been standing right next to me.

"Yes," I said, "I'm fine. Thank you for asking."

He leaned into my shoulder to say something only I could hear,

"I don't believe you," he said, and winked at me.

We kept walking through the corridors when dad and Mr. Pemberton suggested we take a break for a bit of refreshment.

"I'd like to keep exploring, if that's alright with you, Father," Toby said.

"Beth, would you like to join us or stay with Toby," my dad asked.

"I'll stay here," I said.

"Ok we will be at the Hanover Inn right across the green," dad said pointing, "meet us there, but you kids don't be too long, we have a lot more of the campus to see."

My neck was starting to hurt from looking up at the tall windows and all the beautiful books. I longed to read them.

"C'mon," Toby said, "I want to find something."

Toby walked over to the card catalogue and started to walk his fingers through the drawer labeled "D-De".

"What are you looking for?"

"You'll see," he said grinning.

He grabbed a tiny yellow pencil and piece of paper off the nearby oak table and wrote something down.

"We are on a mission," he said.

He walked with such confidence and purpose like he knew the place.

"Where are you going," I whispered as we walked past a long table of students bent over books and notebooks with highlighters and index cards.

Being summer term there were not as many students, but even if the place was empty I felt like an intruder. It was a painful reminder of what I missed at my old school where I had belonged, and yet after just one year at my high school, I already felt transformed, an outsider even here.

Toby raced down the marble steps and took us down a corridor to a narrow door at the end of the hall. Once inside, the air was different. Cooler and sweet smelling.

A middle-aged woman behind the desk looked up and said in a calm voice, "Can I help you?"

"Yes, please," Toby said handing her the slip of paper, "I was hoping you could find this for us."

She smiled and looked at the piece of paper.

"Do you have your professor's permission to see this?"

"No, let me explain," Toby said, and I watched him turn from a silly boy into the most polite, charming man I had ever seen.

He had the comportment and polite manner of speaking as if he were addressing the Queen of England herself. His voice was like music to me.

"Certainly," she said.

He smiled, then winked at me.

The woman opened up a metal grated door and closed it behind her.

The tik, tik, tik of her heels walking up the metal steps now the only sound in the room.

"Go grab a seat over there," he whispered to me.

Behind walls of glass were metal stacks. It was a long room with a single row of long tables in the middle and a big arched window at the end of the room.

She had white gloves on and carried the boxes towards me with Toby just a step behind.

Toby sat in the seat next to me, and she gave us both a pair of gloves.

"Please, put these on," she said.

"Thank you," Toby said, and he put his gloves on with the same controlled eagerness he had taken a second pecan bun this morning at breakfast.

"The last time I wore white gloves was at dancing school," I said.

It was as if my old self, the girl who was not to be a debutante had stepped even lower and was not worthy to sit among those great books or even put on white gloves.

Toby pulled the first of three boxes close to us

and opened it up.

"It's Dante's *Divine Comedy*," he said.

His eyes widened at the three boxes stacked on the table in front of him.

"Illustrated by Salvador Dalí. I wanted to show you."

I did not know what he was talking about. Neither of those names meant anything to me.

He opened the first box which contained the works for *Inferno*. As he was carefully looking through the pages, the librarian brought another box to our table, and then walked back to her station.

"Do you know the art of Dalí," Toby whispered.

"No."

"Have you heard of Surrealism?"

"I overheard George say that word to Lydia one time at Christmas, but I don't know what it is."

"Ok, well, I will show you some art books when we get back to the house,"

The heat of shame, like I should know what Toby was talking about, and I didn't. Like the time I didn't know a word and mom told me to look it up in the dictionary; but I had not yet learned how to use a dictionary.

❈ ❈ ❈

One summer I attempted to read a book of George's that was too advanced for my age. It had elaborate illustrations of knights and castles with many words I could not pronounce, nor understand.

I asked about a word I did not understand.

"We have a dictionary," mom said.

"Can you help me look it up, mommy?"

Mom and dad were sitting there reading their newspapers.

Without looking at me mom spoke from behind the wall of the Providence Journal newspaper.

"You're brother George was reading *War and Peace* at the age of four, surely you can look up a word on your own? Can't you?"

I remember walking over to the large Oxford Dictionary that we kept on a stand, and I had to pull up a chair to be tall enough to reach it.

I looked at the letters and words, but they made no sense to me. I turned page after page in quiet desperation, my anxiety building as I looked for the word I was trying to understand. I felt stupid, and concluded that I just wasn't smart enough to read George's book.

❋ ❋ ❋

Toby had been explaining more about this artist Dalí,

"The project was cancelled," he said, "because it was such a huge scandal."

"Why was it a scandal?"

I didn't even know what he really meant by

that word, scandal, but didn't want to look any more stupid than I already did. A full year at public school had already conditioned me to not ask so many questions; reversing the good practice of inquiry that had been so much encouraged at my old school. I was changing. And not for the better.

"Because Dalí was part of the Surrealist group led by Andre Breton, and they practiced necromancy and other occultist things, like Poe."

I have no idea what you are talking about, and I feel so stupid for not.

"Look at these," he said, "they're exquisite."

Toby looked so happy and excited. This was his treasure and he wanted to share it with me.

I looked at the watercolor in front of him and to me it seemed grotesque and creepy. Like the nightmares I had as a kid of an orange hand emerging from the tuner dial of my sister's radio in our shared bedroom at the summer house. It would go for my armpit, and tickle me endlessly, but when I tried to scream, no sound would come out.

Toby kept smiling, and looking adoringly at these images.

"They are watercolors, see?"

If you can't say anything positive, don't say anything at all.

I nodded.

Toby continued, "Dalí fell in love with Dante's *Divine Comedy* so much so that he continued the project even after the Italian government cancelled his commission. He had faith in the project, and worked at it until he finished. Lucky for him it was picked up by a French publisher who brought it into the world in 1959."

Toby looked at me for my reaction.

"I like the colors," I said trying so hard to understand what it was in these watercolors that he so clearly appreciated.

"Dalí was a true artist. Called a criminal by some, and blasphemous by others, he ignored the opinions of others, and continued the work out of love. Determined to complete it."

The image in front of him was of a distorted half of a man with what looked like a stream of green vomit coming out of his mouth and something splitting his head in two.

I winced. I felt sick to my stomach. My body knew something I didn't want to admit.

It's so ugly. But he's made such an effort to show me this and it's obviously important to him.

Looking at those horrible images, that were regarded as such great art, my body felt so different compared to how it did listening to the Chopin his mother played for us after dinner.

"I don't understand it," I said, "maybe I need to read the book first?"

Toby looked back at the watercolors. I watched his gloved hands move through the images.

It was more than just his hands and wearing Top Siders without socks that reminded me of my brother George. It was a familiar feeling. A heaviness, a darkness that scared me and settled in the pit of my stomach.

With my gloves on, I pulled the last item the librarian had brought to our table.

It was also *The Divine Comedy* but illustrated by a different artist. One named William Blake. Those images looked more realistic to me, even beautiful; and although some were scary, they did not make me viscerally recoil like the other ones did.

I looked over at Toby and he was smiling at a grotesque image of a woman's torso with the long jagged legs of spider.

"We should get going, our dads will surely be looking for us by now," I said.

The afternoon sunlight was now flooding through the arched window at the end of the row of tables. The light made the oak appear more golden and infused the green glass of the table lamps. Glowing emeralds.

I took a deep, silent breath and rested my eyes on the beauty of the light in the room.

I respected Toby and so desperately wanted to appreciate what he was enjoying, but I didn't get it.

With hesitation, Toby carefully put the images back in their respective boxes. The librarian caught my eye and walked over to our table to retrieve the items.

"Thank you so very much," Toby said, "these

are just wonderful."

His expression looked like my heart felt hearing the music of Chopin.

"My pleasure," she said "I'm glad to see a young man that appreciates such great art."

We left the library and strolled across the green of the open quad.

Toby walked with his hands thrust deep in his pants pockets, and when we were mid-way across, he took a deep breath through his nose and turned around,

"Look at this place! It's so grand!"

"Yes," I said, "it certainly is."

He looked like he belonged there, but I didn't feel I did.

Our dads were sitting out on the covered porch and waved at us as we crossed the main street. Beers and sandwiches on the table in front of them.

"You kids order whatever you like," my dad said, "my treat today."

We both ordered club sandwiches. I got a ginger ale and Toby's dad ordered him a dark beer.

Toby told our dads about our adventure and finding the Dalí illustrations.

"Beth wasn't too keen on it, but I think she liked the Blake version," he said looking over at me.

Feeling I had to explain what was surely my ignorance, I said, "I did like Blake and I think I may just need to read the book first to appreciate the illustrations by Dalí."

Toby smiled and asked his father, "Can we make a trip to the campus bookstore after? Maybe we can get Beth properly introduced to Dante."

"I think that's a great idea, son. We shall all go," said Mr. Pemberton.

The campus bookstore was wonderful. I thought of the marked-up books I had to use all year and longed for the days when books were fresh and crisp and mine to write in if I pleased.

I looked for a new copy of *Leaves of Grass* which was the only book I enjoyed that first year and Toby walked over to me with three books. *Inferno*, *Purgatorio* and *Paradiso*.

"I thought it was called *The Divine Comedy*," I said.

"It is - this is it," Toby smiled, "in three volumes. In an English translation of course."

Notebooks, new pens, rows of clean fresh books lined the shelves. I wanted to cry. I missed my school so much.

Dear Joy, you are so lucky to be where you are.

"Ready to go?" Toby asked.

"Yes," I said, "I think I will get this,"

Toby looked at the book I had in my hand and shook his head back and forth.

"Oh, no," he said, "follow me."

He walked us back to the Ws in Poetry and

pulled a different book from the bottom shelf.

"This one," he said handing me a much smaller book, "is from 1855. Best to read it as he *originally* conceived of it. They must have told you Whitman wrote nine versions over the course of his lifetime."

No, I was not taught that. Not at all.

"Thank you," I said.

He nodded towards my hand holding the one I originally picked out.

"Put that one back," he said, "and I will get you the 1855 version, along with your Dante. After-all, everyone must read Dante."

Toby's knowledge and worldliness so much reminded me of George, and yet I felt attracted to him. I wanted to hug him and at the same time I feared how he smiled at those ugly, nightmarish pictures. My feelings were all jumbled and yet something so familiar in the deepest part of me.

His hands held the three books out like a tray and he said,

"C'mon now put Mr. Whitman on top."

I put the 1855 version Toby picked out on top of the Dante books he held out to me and put the other one back on the shelf.

Toby's smile, his hands, all these wonderful books and the bastion of knowledge.

Lunch seemed to make him more animated, playful like he was that morning. I liked him this way and decided to not think about the feeling I got in my stomach back in the Special Collections

Room.

Late that night after dinner, Toby and I got permission to walk the half mile to Lake Overlook Drive.

Dad handed me a flashlight because as he explained,

"The last thing you kids want to run into is a skunk!"

But we didn't really even need it, it was a clear, warm night and the indigo sky was filled with stars.

The road took us to a hilltop clearing where we could see surrounding mountains and look down onto the lake. I had walked there a few times with my parents on our Sunday afternoon walks, but Toby had not seen it before.

It was a clear night and somehow, it seemed even more beautiful because of the day we'd shared.

"See that one there," Toby said tracing the sky with his index finger, "that's Hercules over there. He had to do twelve labors to atone for his sins. Almost sounds Catholic."

Toby's blond hair seemed bright as the sun to me in the light of the stars.

"Are you Catholic?" I asked.

"Sort of, I guess. I was raised in the church. An oddball, I'd say because being English, I should be Anglican but mummy never made it easy."

"What do you mean?"

"My father was raised Anglican, but he had to convert to marry mum in The Church. And then they raised us Catholic."

"You and your sister? The one in the picture?"

"Yeah. Lily, she's my better half. We could be twins if we weren't born four years apart. We have chapel at school and I generally go to the Anglican mass with my friends who are all Anglican."

"Do you believe in God," I asked.

"I guess so, sure" Toby said, and he sat down and laid back on his elbows not taking his eyes off the sky above us.

I sat down next to him.

"I mean, I have been going to Mass ever since I can remember, I used to *really* believe, and I was quite taken with it. Now, it's habit mostly. I don't really think about it too much unless I have to go to confession. Then I *have* to think about all my sins, and all the ways I offend God."

"You have to confess your sins?" I said.

"Yeah," he said, "of course. And often."

I thought really hard about it for a minute.

How many sins have I done? A lot, I'm sure with how mom and dad always scold me.

"We always had Christmas Vespers at my old school before winter break, but besides that, religion never really came up at school."

"Be glad you don't have to go confess your sins. It's horrible," he said, "So, do you believe in God?"

"I do," I said. "I just don't know much. There's

so much I don't know."

"Do you say any prayers?"

"My mom taught me how to say my prayers every night before bed. I always did until we moved here. Heck, I got kicked out of Sunday School when I was six for asking if Jesus' mom was in heaven. And I don't read the Bible."

Toby laughed, "You're a Protestant, and you don't read the Bible?"

"My mother does, but I don't even own one. That's kinda weird, isn't it? I like to sing at church, and love going to service on Christmas Eve, but they don't even make me go every week anymore. Dad used to say I had to go until I was sixteen, but this year he changed it to fifteen, so since my birthday, I sleep-in on Sundays, and when they get home from church, we all read the New York Times and Boston Globe together."

Toby laughed quietly, but not in a mean way.

"What," I said, "what's so funny?"

"Well, I'm thinking that if you got kicked out of Protestant Sunday School when you were just six for asking questions about the Virgin Mary, *and* you don't read the Bible, maybe deep down you already *are* Catholic. You certainly seem to have the guilt for it."

I was afraid he was making fun of me, but he wasn't. He tapped his shoulder into mine.

"I'm just teasing you. It's all rubbish, the church and the priests. You're lucky you don't have to go."

"Look!" Toby said. He pointed up.

"See that? That's a comet!"

We both looked at the night sky, speechless in the face of its beauty.

Then I said,

"That's how I know God exists."

"What do you mean," Toby asked.

"When I see something that amazing, I know there's something much greater. It's when I see all the pain and suffering, that I begin to question."

I told Toby about last summer and the sudden move, about Eric dying, and how terrible I felt about insisting that my sister sleep with me on Christmas Eve when it would be their first and last Christmas eve as husband and wife. I told him about Mr. McG's class and him leaving; about James Allen's suicide, and everything. I confessed to Toby. He put his arm around me; he pulled me close and kissed my forehead and said,

"If I was a priest, and right now I wish I was because I would absolve you."

Few people had held me in my life when I cried: Hope, Dad, and now Toby.

"I don't know anything, Toby. Where do we go when we die? There's so much I don't understand. And no one will tell me what happened."

"It's ok," Toby said and he pulled a cloth handkerchief from his pocket and gave it to me.

"Promise me one thing," he said.

"What," I said.

"Promise me that you will read Dante all the way through. Most people only read the *Inferno*, but you gotta get to *Paradiso*, it's the best part."

"Ok," I said, still messy from crying.

"If you read it by Christmas, then we can talk about it. My parents really like it here, so I'm pretty sure we'll be back for the holiday."

"OK," I said, "I promise."

"We will come right back here in the snow and stand right here under the stars, and talk about Dante. You'll love it, I just know you will. You're a really great girl, and you don't even know that do you?"

And with that he kissed me on my forehead again, then stood up and held out his hand to help me up.

He hugged me for a long time, and then he walked me back to my house, and recited Keats as we walked,

"Bright star! Would I were steadfast as thou art!"

"Toby, shhhh, not so loud," I said feeling embarrassed.

"Why not," he laughed, "even the animals love Keats!"

By the time we got to my house, he had recited the whole poem from memory. He walked me to my door, handed me my dad's flashlight and said goodnight.

I was so happy, my heart felt at peace and full of

joy at the same time. I felt so much better after talking with Toby and the lovely day we'd had together.

I looked at my new books and the excitement I used to have about learning was back.

It was almost midnight when I pulled out the *Inferno*, opened it to Canto I, and began to read:

> *"Midway upon the journey of our life*
> *I found myself within a forest dark,*
> *For the straightforward pathway had been lost."*

The next morning, I woke up much later than usual, and figured I would be having breakfast alone, so I made my slice of toast, sectioned my half of a grapefruit, and sat down with Dante.

Mom walked in from their bedroom with her cup of coffee.

"No reading at the table, young lady."

I sighed audibly, closed the book, and sat it next to my placemat.

She walked over and picked it up.

"What are you reading?"

"Dante's *Divine Comedy*," I said.

I took a bite of toast, and mom sat down at the table reading the description on the back.

"It's the first part, *Inferno*," I said.

"I know what it is," she said, "I've read it."

She sat down and watched me eat my grape-fruit.

My stomach muscles tightened waiting for her to make some comment about my figure when instead she said,

"Your brother George read *The Divine Comedy* in the first grade. He insisted on reading the Italian version and read the whole thing with just an Italian dictionary."

She took a sip of coffee and then asked,

"Are you reading it for school?"

"No, mom," I said, "my new school does not have a summer reading list."

"Is that your father's copy?"

"No," I said.

"I didn't think so. If it was, I was going to say how'd the second-hand man miss that one. It's a very nice copy. The second-hand man got all your father's books, and he probably got Grammy's diary too."

"Oh, no, not Grammy's diary," I said.

The old familiar sadness was seeping back in.

"Where did you get it from," mom said, holding my new book.

"Toby gave it to me."

Her eyes went flat, and her lips thinned.

"Toby? Toby Pemberton gave this to you?"

"Yes."

"Did he let you borrow it from their house? I certainly hope you didn't just take it off the shelf."

"No, mother. It's not from their house."

"Where did you get it from then?"

"When we were at the college bookstore yes-terday. Toby wanted to buy me the *Divine Comedy* and Walt Whitman's *Leaves of Grass*."

"You know better than that," she said, frown-ing, "did you even ask your father if that was alright?"

"What? No," I said, "What have I done wrong?"

"Beth, I want you to return all those books to Toby right after you finish your breakfast. Thank him of course, but then you must tell Toby that you simply cannot accept such a generous gift."

"Why? Why can't I keep them?"

She handed the book to me, looked right in my eyes and said,

"Because young lady, a boy who does some-thing *this nice* for you must be expecting some-thing from you in return."

GREASE TRAPS FOR DANTE

The large man in swim trunks, top siders and a pink Lacoste shirt walked up to the window.

"How much for two scoops of vanilla on a sugar cone?"

"That would be $3.50," I said.

"What?! For two scoops of ice cream on a damn sugar cone? That's highway robbery!"

He spoke loudly. I began to get nervous, then remembered what Ben told me to do when we got a difficult customer: *the customer is always right, give them another option, make them happy.*

"Two scoops in a dish without the cone is only

$2.00," I said, "would you like that instead, sir?"

He paused, looking me over. My anxiety was building at the sight of the line of parents and their kids growing restless behind him.

It was a hot, sunny Saturday in August, and I was the only one on the early shift. That meant I had to prepare the food, scoop the ice cream, and do the math. And I hated the math.

My anxiety must have shown on my face by that point.

He laughed and then said,

"Well, I *own* this place, so I guess it won't break the bank if I get two scoops on a sugar cone for $3.50," he said.

"Very good, sir," I said, "two scoops vanilla on a sugar cone coming right up."

I felt his eyes on me as I wrapped a napkin around the sugar cone, and then leaned into the freezer and scooped out vanilla from the tub. *Is he pulling my leg or is this really "the boss" I had heard about?*

I handed him the cone, and he gave me a five dollar bill.

I rang up $3.50 on the register, and the drawer opened with its bell sound. I put the five dollar bill on top of the other fives, and started to pull his change from the drawer.

"Thanks," he said, licking the dripping vanilla, "this is worth every penny. Keep the change. You should have a tip jar, you know. A young, pretty girl like you will be getting a lot of tips!"

I looked at the counter by the register. We didn't have a 'tip' jar. I would ask Ben about that.

"Thank you," I said, but he was already several feet away, lumbering towards the lake.

The next four hours flew by in a flurry of hot dogs, Cokes, Fanta and ice cream.

It was hard work, but I was determined to read Dante like I promised Toby I would, and since mom made me return the books Toby had given me, I was saving-up to buy my own.

They were paying me .50 cents an hour, so it was going to take time to save, but I was determined. It had been so humiliating when mom made me take those books back. Toby was nice about it, but I could tell he thought it was weird.

The hut was getting hot. Serving cones was better than hotdogs because at least then I could get relief from the freezer opening.

When the line finally cleared, I was so thirsty I grabbed a bottle of Fanta from the fridge. Then stopped.

This will cost me $2.50, that's almost a full shift's pay.

I put the Fanta back in the fridge, and looked at my Mickey Mouse watch. Ben was due to show up for his shift in fifteen minutes, and at that point I could go pee and then go home.

I busied myself wiping down the counters and making sure everything was in order. I pulled more hot dogs from the freezer and put them in the steamer.

"Hey there," a voice said.

It was the man in the pink Lacoste shirt.

"Hi, what can I do for you?"

"It's what I can do for you," he said, "I've been watching you. You're a hard worker, very polite and good with the customers. How would you like a real job?"

"A real job?"

"Yes, in the restaurant," he said, and pointed to the club house.

My parents and I ate dinner there when we first arrived a year ago. I had been in such shock I could not even remember eating. What I remembered was how concerned mom was that dad drank not just two but three gin and tonics. One before dinner and a second one with dinner and a third with dessert.

"I'm only 15," I said, "don't I have to be older to work there?"

He waved his hand at me, "Nah, you won't be a cocktail waitress," he said.

His eyes lingered somewhere below my face.

"Although I am sure you would do very well at that."

He looked at my face again and continued, "No, you would be our dishwasher."

"Dishwasher?"

"Yeah, it's easy, we have a machine, you just stack 'em, rack 'em and shove 'em in. Then pull them out. Real easy work, and much better pay."

My eyes brightened at the thought of making more money. More money meant I would be reading Dante sooner.

"How much does it pay?"

"$2.00 an hour," he said, "that's a hellofalot more than you are getting now, isn't it?"

"Yes," I said, "when can I start?"

"How 'bout tonight?"

"Would it be alright if I went home and changed first? I smell like hamburger grease and hotdogs."

He laughed again, and put out his meaty hand for me to shake through the "Orders Here" window.

"Sure that's fine," he said, "come back at 4:30, ask for the manager Brenda, and she will show you the ropes."

I shook his hand, "Thank you sir, thank you!"

I rode my bike home; told mom about the job; and quickly showered and changed. Mom had made me a tuna fish sandwich.

I gobbled down the first half, and excitedly explained the job to her.

"Don't talk with your mouth full," she said.

"It's a lot more than I am making now," I said and swallowed down some milk.

She did not seem too thrilled.

"A dishwasher?"

Her nose went up a bit.

"When your brother George was your age, during the summers he made money tutoring underprivileged children. And on the weekends, he crewed on the Commodore's Yacht. They won many races that summer thanks to your brother."

I wish I could be sailing on Narraganset Bay right now. I miss Kim and those thrilling days long ago that I got to crew for her. What was it Kim always told me, don't be afraid to try new things?

My face got hot. The familiar pain returned. It was no use, I would never be as good, as smart or as handsome as George. He was fourteen years older than me. I would never catch-up to perfect, All-Ivy, George.

I was hungry, but after mom's words, I had trouble swallowing my sandwich. I chewed a few more bites in silence, when she said,

"Well, dear, maybe it will be better for you. At least you won't be tempted to eat that ice cream. You don't want to get fat."

Mom was referring to a story I told her a few weeks before - the time a customer changed their mind on a flavor. They had chosen Peppermint Stick.

"No, make it chocolate," Ben had said.

I had already scooped one scoop of Peppermint Stick into a cone.

"What do I do with this?"

"You can throw it out, or eat it if you want to," he had said.

So I took a bite of the Peppermint Stick ice cream I held in my hand.

"Not now," Ben scolded, "not in front of the customers!"

I set it down in a dish by the register. By the time I got back to it, ten minutes later, it was a cone drowning in ice cream soup, so I threw it out.

I felt so bad that I made a mistake, and I made it worse by telling mom about it. Now she thought I ate ice cream cones all day, every day.

That afternoon, at 4:30 sharp, I met Brenda, and she showed me around the restaurant. She introduced me to the waiters, the cocktail waitress, the bus boy and the cook.

Shelly the cook had some music playing quietly. The kitchen was far enough away that she could play it in a small cassette player on the shelf without it being heard by the customers.

The dishwasher was in a corner. A big metal box with a large sink to left, and metal surfaces on either side of the doors.

My shift was spent in this L-shaped location dumping food into the trash; spraying off the plates; stacking plates, glasses and cups vertically into racks to the left of the machine. Push them in; bring down the massive metal doors; wait until the light turned green; lift the doors, and pull the racks of dishes out on the right side; and put them away. The machine was so fast! Much faster than helping mom do dishes at home one at a time!

My first night I messed up. Brenda became irritated with me when she saw me dump a half-eaten plate of food into the trash.

"What are you doing? Take the uneaten dinner roll off the plate, and put it back in the bread basket. It's still good."

This grossed me out.

I looked over at Billy, the twenty-something waiter, and he shrugged.

From then on, I checked the plates and baskets for uneaten bread, and put it back like I was told to.

I got to wear a white jacket made out of heavy cotton, and I liked that I didn't have to worry about getting water or food on my clothes.

I liked the rhythm and flow of the work and the physicality of being a dishwasher. When it was busy, the time flew by. Best of all, it did not require a lick of math!

I also liked all the music Shelly played. Before that summer, I had never even heard of Bonnie Raitt.

On Saturday nights, after closing, during clean-up, Shelly played the song *I Thank You* and we would sing to each other and dance around the kitchen.

Saturdays after closing Brenda and the waiters would sit at the bar, counting tips and sipping cocktails.

One night she offered me a sip of her drink.

"No thank you," I said, "goodnight," and I

turned to leave.

I turned back again to look when I heard a funny sound and saw she had something like a cocktail straw up her nose as she leaned over he mahogany bar.

What is that?

"Hey Kid," she said, wiping her nose.

"I have a special project for you. I want you to show-up at 3:30 tomorrow, ok?"

"Sure," I said.

What they were doing made me nervous. She laughed as I walked out the door. I was sure they were laughing at me.

The next day, I showed up early for my Sunday shift, just like she'd asked.

She looked pretty rough. Her long hair hung around her big glasses like the pictures of Janis Joplin that I saw on the wall of Lydia's bedroom when I was little.

"Reporting for duty," I said smiling, hoping I could help her feel better.

She walked to the back, and waved at me to follow her. Then she handed me a large bucket, and one of the big spatulas they used in the industrial sized bread machine.

"I need you to empty the grease trap," she said.

"It's downstairs, in the men's locker room, in the wall between the two showers. You'll see it."

"Now go. Afterwards just dump it in parking lot trash bin. Rinse out the bucket; and then bring the bucket and spatula back here."

The club house restaurant was in the same building as the pool, sauna and locker rooms. I walked out into the dining room which was empty because it was between the lunch and dinner hour. Billy was vacuuming. I headed down the hallway by the pool and down the stairs to the locker rooms.

I knocked on the men's locker room door. Hearing nothing, I opened it slowly. I was nervous. At first it looked just like women's locker room, a mirror image with two showers, bathroom stalls, sinks. Then I saw the difference: urinals. The women's room did not have urinals, and I had never seen one before.

I walked over to the two shower curtains facing each other and stood on the wooden planks between them and sat the bucket and spatula down. On the wall I saw the outline of a metal door with a small pull-ring on it.

I pulled the ring and the door dropped open with a long, metal rectangular box inside full of waxy yellow and brown gunk.

The smell made me gag, and I stepped back.

"Oh God," I said, involuntarily, "Gross!"

How would I get this out? Scoop it out?

With the door opened at a 45 degree angle, I pulled on the top metal ridges of the deep, rectangular box. I pulled it out and held it over the bucket. It was in a metal sleeve and when I pulled it out, the sides were open, exposed showing the grease had formed a block of dense fat.

Then I noticed it was moving. I let go out of shock and it dropped into the bucket.

It was moving because it was full of grease, and rotting food, and white squirming maggots!

Maggots!!

"Hello?" I heard a low voice.

"Hello. Someone's in here." I yelled back towards the door. I panicked remembering a man might need to use the locker room while I am in here.

"I can see that," the voice said entering the room.

I stood up and began wiping off the front of my white dishwasher's jacket.

A boy about my age in running shorts, white socks and sneakers walked towards me.

"Can I help you," he said.

Something moved under my hand. I wanted to scream and jump out of this coat.

Don't be such a baby!

I swallowed my scream and smiled at the boy trying my best to compose myself.

"Sorry I am in here, I will be done in a moment."

He looked behind me at the wall and the bucket, and stepped closer to me.

"Grease trap?" he said.

"Yes," I said, "they asked me to clean it, but I have never done it before."

He leaned over and looked into the bucket.

"Cool," he said.

"It's gross!" I said.

"Let me help you," he said, "I will hold it, and you scrape it out. Don't worry, they won't crawl on you if I am holding it for you."

He lifted the rectangular block of grease up by the metal edge and I placed the spatula into the grease. It was dense.

"Ewww!"

The smell was so foul, I held my breath and ran the spatula along the long edge of the frame.

The block of grease and maggots slowly slopped into the bucket.

The boy laughed and said,

"That's a lot of hamburgers, or steak. Or bacon. What do you think it was?"

He leaned in looking down into the bucket.

"I don't know," I said, "I just know I never, ever, *ever* want to eat in this restaurant again."

We both laughed.

He took the spatula from me, and scraped out the remains. I got up to wash my hands and wiped a glob of grease off my sleeve.

He slid the metal frame back into the long metal box, and then pushed it closed back into the wall.

"I will dump this out for you," he said holding the bucket in one hand and the spatula in the other.

For the first time, I really looked at him. He was skinny but very muscular. A runner, and I realized he looked familiar.

"My name's Scott by the way. You're Beth, right?"

"How - "

"We take the same bus together."

"Oh, yes," I said starting to ramble, "we just moved here last summer. I will be a Sophomore this fall."

"And I will be a junior," he said.

I recognized his face then. His big Roman-esque nose and soft brown eyes. Usually he wore jeans and a flannel shirt. I suddenly felt embar-rassed realizing how little he was wearing now.

His eyes focused on something on my front, and I got self-conscious.

He smiled and said, "All clear. No maggots on you."

He carried the bucket out, and I followed him. His back was tanned golden brown, but his neck and arms were even darker, like he worked out-side. The hair on his neck was wet with sweat. His shorts looked dry except for a sweat stain where the waistband met his lower back.

We walked outside into the sunlight. It was a beautiful day and the air smelled fresh.

"Are you a runner," I asked as he hoisted the bucket over the trash bin and emptied it out.

"Yeah, cross country. I like to run to here from my house and back for training. It's a good six miles each way, and lots of hills."

He handed me the bucket and spatula.

"I always like to use the men's room at the half-way point, and get some water. It's really nice here with the lake too."

I stood there, stupidly forgetting what I had to do next.

"You might want to rinse that out over there," he said, and pointed to the outdoor spigot.

"Thank you, for your help," I said, "And nice to meet you."

"Nice to meet you Beth, good luck. I'm sure I'll see ya round."

And with that he headed back towards the clubhouse, and I rinsed the bucket and spatula in a daze, smiling.

LETTERS,
LETTERS,
LETTERS

<u>Saturday, September 20th, 1980</u>

Dear Toby,
Guess what? I finally got back to reading Dante!
I am reading about Aristotle, Plato and Ovid in
Limbo right now. Then I decided I had to write
you.

Isn't Ovid the poet you recommended I read too?
Why are they in Limbo and not heaven? I wish
you were here to discuss it with me. I think all
poets should be in heaven automatically. What

do you think?

Did you get to sail along the coast of Scotland like you wanted to? I asked about going to school where you are. Not a chance for that. They want me under their roof. But mom and dad did finally have a meeting with my guidance counselor about French. Just for me, the teacher will allow me to do Independent study all year.

The counselor told my dad that a student of my background was "good" for the school, something about how the teachers consistently say I "add a lot to class discussions" and that I am an asset. An asset? I had never heard that before.

Dad was so pleased, all the way home, he went on and on about "giving back" and at the same time how I should "count my blessings" and never think I was better than anyone else.

How can I be an asset and at same time think I am exactly the same? I don't understand my parents. You are so lucky you get to go to boarding school. I miss my old school so much. I must admit to feeling a bit jealous. I hope you understand. Do you ever get jealous?

Of course on the way home mom had to lecture me on it too. "Don't let what she said go to you head, remember pride cometh before a fall." Jeeze she says that every time I even look in the mirror to check if my blouse is buttoned right. Mom is tough as nails, nails wrapped in a mink coat that is.

So that meeting was back before Labor Day, and guess what? You won't believe it. <u>Just this week</u>, my guidance counselor said that<u> she is leaving</u> after Fall Term to work at the same private school that I asked about transferring to!!!! I can't believe it. So I have to stay to "be an asset to the school?" But she goes on to work at the school I begged dad to let me go to? So I guess I am stuck. I hate it. I wish we could talk on the phone, mom says it's too expensive.

I think my dad was a bit surprised by the news of my guidance counselor taking a job at that other school. He said nothing when I told him, and the next day he asked me if I thought we should get a puppy. I think it might be his way to cheer me up a bit. Well, it worked.

So we are going to the animal shelter today!! I will drop this letter in the mail to you on the way. Wish me luck on finding a good dog. I doubt they will have puppies, but here's hoping.

Anyway, like you always say, I need to crack-on and not get too down about school. At least now I have Dante to read, and your letters to look for-

ward to.

And I also just found out about a book called Cosmos by Carl Sagan. Have you read it? A boy named Scott sits with me on the bus some mornings and he's reading it. He said it's really good and there's a TV special too, but we don't have a TV (as you already know). Scott said I could borrow his book when he's done reading it. Let me know if you have read that. I want to know what you think.

Are you playing rugby again this year? That seems like such a wicked game. We don't have that here. Do girls ever get to play it or is it only for boys? I think I might try out for ski team this year. Sounds fun, right?

Let me know what's going on for you.

I have enclosed a funny comic from the Boston Globe Sunday paper that I thought you might enjoy.

Fondly,
Beth

* * *

21.10.80
Edinburgh

Dear Beth,

Thanks for your letter. Yes! We did go on a grand adventure! For seven days we sailed the North Sea! I even got to skipper for a day. It was hard, wet and cold but fun. The weather was a bit rough and we had to wear full gear the whole time.

We sailed the school yacht several miles out, and made a triangle heading down to Robin's Hood Bay and then sailed up the coast. We learned how to navigate like Galileo - using a sextant and the moon, sun and stars.

I thought about sailing with you that windy day on the lake. At dinner one night, I told the guys about our little adventure. I told them about the crazy winds and white caps on the lake that day, and the look on your face when you turned around after you heard me yell, "I've lost the boat!!" And there you were standing on the bow - with the boat sailing away from the dock I was supposed to land us at.

Of course, they thought that was hilarious. I told them what a good sport you were - how you calmly lowered the mainsail, jumped overboard and then swam that damned Blue Jay to the dock where I stood like a Monty Python village idiot. Telling this story was a big mistake because they ribbed me for the whole trip about it. Even our captain jumped in on the jokes.

Patrick amused himself and everyone else when he yelled mockingly from the bow, "Hey Toby, lose something? I've lost the spinnaker!"

One afternoon, when I was at the helm sailing us through rough seas, they all acted like a bunch of girls and began screaming in high-pitched voices over the roar of the waves, "Oh Toby, *please don't* lose the boat!"

Such tossers - all of them. I am sorry to say that, but I hope you don't think me sissy for preferring your company over those sods.

Anyway - I would love to take you sailing some day on a real yacht - on the ocean...There are lots of adventures I want to have with you. You are on my mind *every* day. I wish you could attend school here.

Of course, I agree! A poet like Ovid should be in heaven! And yes he is the one I said you must read. Specifically, read *Metamorphosis* first then his love poems.

In my literature class we are reading ALL of Dickens in the order of publication. I am also taking two art classes this term, sculpture AND painting. I enjoy them both tremendously. My dad is not any too thrilled about my interest in fine art, but he told me that I could apply to study in France and Italy for the summer. So I will be applying to the Sorbonne for the summer of '81. The bad news is that if I get accepted, I won't see you for awhile, not until *next* Christmas! Can you believe it? It will be Christmas 1981 when I see you again. I know that's over a year away, but we can write just like we promised. Wish me luck! I have to create a portfolio to send in when I apply, so I have to do that in addition to *all* my classes plus sport and sailing. I will be very busy, but never too busy to write you *mon petit chou*!

Thank you for the comic, I pinned it right next to my desk. Send me a picture of you! Would you? I have the ones we took last summer, but they are mostly far away. If you get school pictures taken this fall, please send me one. I will send you one of me too.

My sister <u>finally</u> made up her mind on school. I thought she was going to bum around the world for another year! I guess she's going to Brown instead of Oxford. She said she wants to focus on music, following in mother's footsteps to be a classical pianist.

Keep on in school. I know you don't like it, but don't give up, you are really smart. Your guidance counselor was right about that!

To answer your question - the answer is yes, I have been jealous before. Usually around sport like now it's around rugby which you also asked about. This guy Patrick (the same one who teased me non-stop on the sailing trip) is a perfect athlete. He is strong, fast and so nimble - and when he gets really hurt, he wears his wounds like a badge of honor. He even refused to tape his ears until the coach had to threaten him about it. I hate him, but honestly it's just because I'm jealous. When I get hurt in rugby - which happens a lot these days - I want to cry - I don't - but I want to - and I hate myself for it, and I am jealous of him being so tough. It's bloody *Lord of The Flies* out there. Patrick - what a bloody bastard I <u>hate him</u>. Anyway, I shouldn't complain. I do still love rugby even if I my face looks like a pumpkin in December after a game.

This is sure to cheer you: But you <u>can't say anything to anyone</u>. Promise?

+++ Sign Here to Promise _____ *+++*

I know you keep secrets like a vault so here it is: Prince Charles will get married next year!!!! One of my teachers at school plays polo with him and apparently there was some new dish at a match that he is quite smitten with. Her name is Lady Diana Spencer. She's a lot younger than he is, but they look really happy. Of course, I had to ask my dad about it, because he knows Charles personally, and he confirmed that it's true!! He grilled me about how honorable it is to keep a secret. No formal announcement has been made yet. All hush, hush, you know.

Of course like Lord Byron, now that I wrote this down, I do request you to burn this letter so that no one else can ever read those words. If I get in trouble with the Royal Family, dad would surely not let me go to France or Italy next summer!!

Write soon, and send me a picture of your smile - I miss you!

~ Ever Yours, Toby

P.S. Yes, I have heard of Carl Sagan, his book, and the TV series Cosmos. I am not sure we will see that over here as it broadcasts on American television, but we have been talking about the book in my Astronomy class.

❋ ❋ ❋

Letters, Letters, Letters. We wrote back and forth like this for months. Toby's handwriting always in tight small print while I tried to write in my neatest cursive which generally didn't work too well.

Getting mail back and forth between New Hampshire and Scotland took time, but we wrote every two weeks, and sometimes I would receive two of his letters on the same day.

We sent each other pressed leaves in the fall, and flowers in the spring. (I pressed mine nicer than he did, sometimes he didn't put them in waxed paper and they arrived dead and crumbly, but still, it was neat).

Sometimes he sent me a coaster from a pub he went to in Edinburg or copied out a poem he especially liked.

For Christmas 1980, he sent me a small, green, leather-bound book of Keats poetry published in 1865 that he found at a "dusty, old" bookstore. For my 16th birthday, he sent me an illustrated copy of *Ars Amatoria* by Ovid.

Mom did not insist that I return these gifts which surprised me especially since Ovid was a bit steamy. I think she was beginning to like Toby. Or at least she approved of him writing to me.

When Prince Charles and Lady Diana Spencer got engaged in February of 1981, I knew it was going to happen before anyone else!

Having delicious secrets to share with each other, things that Toby trusted me with, and things I trusted him with made me feel closer to him.

We wrote to each other about *everything*, and our letters over the months became increasingly intimate so much so that almost every letter ended with "//LBR" after our signature which was our secret shorthand for "per Lord Byron Request - burn this letter after reading".

I started to feel like I was falling in love with him, but we lived so far apart. *How would it work?* I told myself to stop being so silly, after all, we hadn't even kissed.

And then there was this nice boy Scott I'd met who sat with me on the bus some days, and asked me to be his date for his junior prom when I was a sophomore. When I told Toby about that, and asked him if he thought I should go with Scott, he only responded, "Sure, that sounds grand." So then I thought maybe Toby didn't like me like I liked him.

I accepted Scott's invitation to the prom, but told him it would just be as friends, and it was a lovely night. Scott was so sweet and kind and held the door for me and everything, a perfect gentleman, but I kept wondering about Toby! It was so confusing.

Toby was accepted at the Sorbonne in Paris for the summer of 1981, and he wrote me letters in June and July, and then the letters stopped.

I got worried. I knew he was very busy and

would be traveling too, but then I imagined a host of possible reasons.

He had told me about his classes and had even sent me some of the sketches he did in his life drawing class. He wrote:

> Just like Vincent van Gogh in 1886! I am drawing nude models in an atelier - a real apprentice - training in the same way so many great artists have in centuries past!

He explained how they would draw naked models for hours at a time. As Toby wrote to me: the models were trained and would hold the pose, *perfectly graceful and perfectly still*.

Sometimes they would do series sketches fast, to warm-up with a pose lasting only one, two or three minutes. Other times, she would hold a long pose.

After an hour or so, the master artist would say to the model, "Bien. Bon temps pour se resposer". At which point she would don her robe, and refresh with a sip of wine or water. Sometimes she would talk with the master artist, but mostly she would be keep to herself. On the days when it was exceptionally hot she would take a quick sponge bath in the restroom.

Then when break was over, the students would return to their easels circled around the model; she would drop her robe, and resume her pose exactly as before.

Toby's drawings were quite good, and I could

tell from them that the women he was drawing were very beautiful.

One in particular I especially liked was the one he had captioned "Ophelia's Dilemma".

I was amazed at how with just a single pencil Toby could make the image look three dimensional. The drawing made me feel happy because it was so beautiful and Toby drew it with his own hand. I touched the paper carefully so as to not smudge the lead, but to touch where his hand had been.

Toby wrote about how moved he was on a particularly hot day in July. When I read it, I didn't know it would be his last letter.

> ... she held a pose and expression like Daphne of Bernini's *Apollo and Daphne*. She was facing me, with the light through the windows angled above and behind her. I watched her become a statue in real time. Her skin as white and perfect as Bernini's smooth marble Daphne, but she breathes and blinks; her nipples as pink as rose petals; her cheeks flushed in the afternoon heat.

> I felt something larger than myself in that room, something universal, like how Plato described beauty reflects our soul's desire for the eternal and an awareness of the divine. Something eternal, universal, common to all humans. And then without warning, I became overhwelmed, and my tears came. I kept drawing with tears silenly seeping.

> It was...something happened. It wasn't sexual mind you, (and I know we talk about all *that*, - you know I would tell you).

> No, this was <u>different,</u> something bigger, like a secret of the universe opened in that very moment,

when the dusty shaft of light shone down on her translucent skin.

Ethereal, it was.

I wish you had been there to see it, Beth. I wish you had been standing there drawing at the easel right next to me.

All the spirits in that room that afternoon: Plato, Bernini, van Gogh, and you and me. We are the same. We don't just see beauty. We feel it, and in its presence, we recognize our soul's desire for the connection to the divine. Like that night last summer when we saw a shooting star.

I had put his sketches on the walls of my room. I could see in such a short time, how his drawing had improved. It made me feel sad because it reminded me how much I had loved my drawing classes I took from Trish at RISD when I was little; and how I always had art classes every year at my old school. How much I longed to be doing what he was.

When the letters stopped, his drawing "Ophelia's Dillemma" made me worry, because it was the last one I received, and because I started to wonder about how beautifully he rendered her. I realized she was the same model who had also posed as Daphne.

He captured the ethereal quality he wrote about. He rendered her more beautifully than the other drawings he sent - did that mean he had feelings for her?

Sometimes an artist's work reveals more about the artist than the subject.

Trish used to say all the time. Now that I was older, it made sense to me - in a new way: my body was awakening to the sensuality of our letters, of his drawings and of life in general.

Maybe the drawing was so beautiful not only because she is beautiful, but also that is how Toby sees her. Maybe something else happened in that July afternoon that he described.

I wrote him back twice in August. First thanking him for the drawings, and then telling him all about my summer job picking strawberries, squash and zucchini at a nearby farm. I wrote him that although I liked the dishwasher job the summer before, this was better because I got a wicked tan, and mom said I lost weight from all the exercise. And I found out I really like strawberries - especially the ones that grow as big as your palm.

Toby's letters about Paris were so romantic. I ached to go there. He described walking along the Seine like so many artists did before him. He walked and drank and ate in the same places as Hemingway, Joyce and Gertrude Stein. He told me about the writers, but what he loved most were the "fine artists". He became obsessed with the bronze sculptures of Rodin and Picasso, and the paintings of Modigliani.

He sent me his thoughts on napkins and drawings from the cafés and the streets of Paris with captions like: *I am sketching this at Deux Magots - sitting in the same place Hemingway did!*

He left roses at Chopin's grave in Pére Lachaise, and sent me a book of correspondance between Chopin and George Sand whom at first I assumed was a man! I soon learned she was an amazing writer who dressed in men's clothes and took a masculine pen name so she could get published supporting herself and her two children.

With each letter I had received, my desire grew. To see what Toby was seeing, and experience it as he did.

As usual with Toby, I always imagined that his life was ten times bigger, better and grander than mine could ever be. Now I was sure of it.

In the absence of his letters, my fears and worry grew, and I drove myself nuts with all reasons I imagined for why his letters stopped coming.

Maybe he finds me boring now.

Is her name really Ophelia? Or was it just his idea to caption his drawing that way given his love of Shakespeare? What did he mean by it?

A zillion different scenarios went through my mind.

Had I done something wrong?

Maybe he really was upset that I went to the prom with Scott even though it was just as friends; and he had said he thought it grand.

He had been so consistent in his writing for almost a whole year, and said he would always find time to write me.

Mon petit chou.

Would he ever lie to me?

What if he was hurt?

That one I quickly put out of my mind because I knew his parents would certainly tell mine if something bad had happened to him.

I wasn't sure when, or if, I would ever hear from him again. I became increasingly sad.

Rumination and doubt set-in.

I will never be a debutante.

Everything took on more meaning. Even music seemed to conspire against me. In August of 1981, the number one song was *Endless Love* which made me think of Toby and me one minute; and what I imagined Toby and the French model to be like the next.

Dad noticed too that Toby's letters had stopped. Whenever *Endless Love* came on the car radio (which was all the time), I would ask him to turn it off. He would turn it off, and then try to reassure me. *I'm sure Toby is just very busy. Try not to worry.*

I re-read the dozens of letters Toby sent since last summer, and looked at his drawings and imagined him with *her.* I imagined she was French (of course), and how they would drink wine, walk the streets of Paris in the evening together, and make love in her garret all though the night. Toby was not a virgin, he had told me about his first time, so I knew it was possible.

Trish's words from long ago played over and

over in my head, *sometimes an artist's work reveals more about the artist than the subject.*

That familiar pain came back. It was like I could feel him going away. I felt all lost again without Toby.

Pitch, yaw & roll.

By September, I could no longer appreciate the beauty of Toby's drawings. I carefully stacked them so as not to smudge them. I put them in the box with all his letters, and put the box deep in my bedroom closet.

"Ophelia's dilemma" the drawing I had loved so much had become a sad reminder of the abrupt absence of Toby. The absence of his voice on the page I had come to depend on and love; and that pain was larger because it sat on top of the pain from all my previous losses:

Grammy, Paige, Joy, Susan, Maggie, my old school, daddy's library, music, art classes, gymnastics, Christmas Vespers, all my teachers, Eric, and Christmases with Little Will, Benji and Hope.

I wanted more dinosaurs, more snow angels.

I started to believe that what Lydia had said after Eric died was true, *everything and everyone you ever love will be taken from you.*

I felt sad.

And old.

Older than I thought I should feel at just 16.

DORIAN'S QUARTERBACK

I asked him, "Do you want me to call a priest for you?"

"No," he said, "I may have been raised Irish Catholic, but just because Oscar Wilde had a deathbed confession, does not mean that I..."

His voice trailed off.

I remembered that day in class two years ago when he told us about Walt Whitman, Alan Ginsburg and himself when he was big, bold and strong.

I got up from the wooden chair next to his Lazy Boy recliner, and put the book I had been reading to him back on the shelf.

So. Many. Books.

Shelves upon shelves made of pine planks on bricks.

I put *The Picture of Dorian Gray* back on the shelf between *The Portrait Of A Lady* and *De Profundis*.

I ran my hands along the spines on the shelf above.

Homer, *The Iliad*.

Plato, *Phaedrus*.

E.M. Forster, *Maurice*.

Jack Kerouac, *On The Road*.

William S. Burroughs, *Naked Lunch*.

Jack Kerouac, *Dharma Bums*.

Steinbeck, *Grapes of Wrath*.

Alan Ginsburg, *Howl*.

Walt Whitman, *Leaves Of Grass*.

Thou shalt not covet. I was coveting his library. Not these books per se, but it was what they represented:

The comfort and security of my father's library that I studied in surrounded by classics on mahogany shelves behind leaded glass doors.

Kept company by *Nancy Drew*, *The Hardy Boys* and *The Chronicles of Narnia* among the thousands of other books that William Jr., George and Lydia had already read and I knew I would grow into.

Saturday mornings with dad taking me to the Providence Atheneum where we would browse the tall stacks together.

Books reminded me of my lost childhood and the knowledge and educational rigor I loved. My old school, my old friends. The life and future I'd lost.

The pain of my parents selling everything and our sudden move to New Hampshire in July of '79 still gnawed greedily at my insides.

And I would not learn the real reason why we moved for years.

Standing there that fall afternoon in front of Mr. McG's books stacked in random order on pine and brick bookshelves, it was as if I knew my future. In that moment without seeing it.

I had the sense of it.

The past and the future folding in on that moment.

Then I felt guilty.

Guilty for having self-pity when I was in the room of a man who was sick with some mysterious "gay cancer" no one knew much about yet.

Guilty for so much.

Toby was right, I wasn't Catholic, but like he said, I sure already had enough of the guilt for it.

I felt eyes at my back.

"You want to borrow something, take it home? You can bring it back next time you visit."

I pulled down Walt Whitman's *Leaves Of Grass*. It was the same version he had us read in class. I flipped though the book and saw pages crammed with annotations of stars, underlines and margin notes like this one:

"Possible Lineage: Plato-> Whitman -> Wilde ->Ginsburg."

Splotches and smears of fountain pen ink. I was hungry for his knowledge, and had so many questions.

For a second the excitement of sharing with him what Toby taught me about all the editions Whitman published during his lifetime filled me.

I turned around to face him, but then I froze when I saw how the tan and brown Lazy Boy recliner seemed to swallow Mr. McG's frame.

This man I respected and was so intimidated by was now a mere shadow of his former self.

Don't be so selfish.

I put Whitman back on the shelf, cleared my throat and said,

"Thank you that is very kind. I might, but not today. What...what about your family? Don't you want them here?"

"What family," he said.

"Your mom?"

"She's dead."

"Your dad?"

"Not a chance in hell."

He picked at the cloth pills on his blanket, and

then with a burst of energy pushed his legs down on the recliner and swiveled away from me.

So much has happened.

So much I didn't know.

But he was no longer a teacher, and I was no longer his student.

Or so I thought.

I moved back to the wooden chair next to him and sat down. Hundreds of dust motes drifted in the shaft of light that fell between us.

Then his voice cracked in a dry whisper,

"Hope Elizabeth Lawrence, what name do you go by these days? Is it Beth still... or... did you ever figure that out?"

"No, it's Beth," I said, "still just Beth."

"Well," he said, "I would like to call you Hope. Would that be ok if I called you Hope?"

"Sure," I said, "that's fine. In fact, I like it."

I thought of the bracelet Hope sent me last Christmas, inscribed with our shared name, *Hope*, and her soft voice over the phone, "It's your name too, you should ask people to call you that if it's what you want."

Now she was gone too.

There would be no more Christmas gatherings with William Jr., Hope, Little Will and Benji.

Those days were gone.

And I missed her and Little Will so much.

I want more dinosaurs, more snow angels.

"Hope," he said, "it suits you."

I looked around the room.

It was getting darker.

The fall afternoon sunlight weakened its reach between two thick burgundy velvet curtains.

"Can I read you anything else?"

"Not right now."

"Is there anything I can get you? A glass of water?"

I desperately wanted him to give me another task.

I didn't know where to rest my eyes or what to do.

I had so many questions I wanted to ask.

Stop it. That would be rude.

Something told me to just be there. To help any way I could, and not ask questions.

Just be there.

It would be in these precious afternoons that fall and winter that I learned how to just be there.

And listen and wait.

As if he read my mind, he laughed and said,

"What I *really* want is a stiff drink but sadly there is no liquor in *this* house."

My face went hot, my feet cold. *How can I get that? I am underage.* I thought of Tommy who was known for getting beer, wine, hard liquor or anything else the students wanted.

Mr. McG laughed.

"I'm just kidding," he said, "no need to panic, though a cup of hot tea would be nice."

"Milk or sugar?"

"Yes," he said, "both."

He pointed and said,

"The kitchen is down that hallway second door on the left."

His forearm was half the girth of what I had remembered, and had two purple spots the size of quarters that shone through his thinning red hair.

He rolled down his sleeves and buttoned the cuffs.

I jumped up and headed to the kitchen with purpose.

Tea, with milk and sugar, that I knew how to do. Smiling I remembered how Toby's mother taught me how to make the perfect "British" cup of tea.

His faint voice behind me, "Run the water for a minute and dump out what's in the kettle."

"OK!"

The kettle was just like mom's: Revere Ware with the copper bottom except hers always looked sparkling brand new.

I found a dried-out sponge and soap under the sink, dumped out the kettle and scrubbed it clean best I could.

I filled the kettle, and put it on the small stove.

This was not a place I ever imagined Mr. McG would live.

The books yes, but everything else did not match how I imagined it would be.

The tough teacher who had made such an impression on me Freshman year in High School was a big red-headed Santa Claus with beefy forearms, thick hands, a booming deep voice and a sharp New York accent.

Intimidating and direct in his speech, and imposing in size to match.

I went over to the fridge to get out the milk, and there was a framed black and white picture on the wall.

James Allen.

Beautiful James Allen.

There he was.

James Allen, smiling in his football uniform. It was the same picture that had been in the yearbook the year he died.

I looked closer and realized it was not a cutout from the yearbook, but it was the original black and white photo that was used for the yearbook. Framed below the picture written in neat calligraphy were these words:

> *James Allen, star quarterback.*
> *Loved my many, and missed by*
> *all those who knew you and those*
> *who will come to know of your*
> *legacy. Number 13 will always be*
> *yours. Rest In Peace, dear boy.*

* * *

The Number 13 football jersey was retired the year he died, and never used by another player.

His parents, brother and girlfriend all spoke at commencement, but his cause of death was not mentioned.

He was remembered for his big smile, friendship and outstanding athleticism.

James Allen.

When his girlfriend got up to speak, she could barely talk, but what she said was beautiful.

I thought of my sister losing her husband, Eric.

I thought how some people take a part of the living with them when they go, and those left behind are never the same.

I wish I had known James Allen better than I did.

In a way he seemed almost God-like, too ethereal for anyone to ever get close enough to really know him.

I smiled with the memory of his voice, and how whenever he saw me, he would consistently make a point of greeting me with his smiling nod and in his New Hampshire accent he'd say, "Well, hello."

And always, even though teachers and students and staff knew who he was, it was the same at every class rollcall:

"James Allen?"

"Hee ya."

For two weeks after James Allen died, Mr. Fisk

would still call his name in Biology during attendance, and there was an echo the silence, as if we all could still hear James Allen respond, "hee ya."

And we could all miss hearing him say it at the same time.

Finally registration printed out a new attendance sheet without James Allen's name listed at all so that Mr. Fisk would no longer call his name.

James Allen.

His long legs always in Levi's denim striding down the hallways with such purpose.

His haystack blond bangs and penetrating blue eyes that always seemed to look right through me.

A look that would unsettle me and comfort me at the same time.

I don't think I was special. I think he made all the girls feel that way when he looked at them.

And perhaps the boys too.

When he looked at you he made you feel that you were the most special person in the world.

* * *

I leaned into the photo, and I whispered,

"Who were you really James Allen? I wish I knew you."

Mr. McG's voice came into the kitchen from behind me,

"Find everything ok?"

Startled, I spun around almost dropping the milk carton at my feet.

"Where do you keep your sugar?" I asked shutting the refrigerator door.

"Up there," he said.

I grabbed the sugar dish and the brown mug next to it from the third shelf.

"If you want to join me there is a second mug in the dishwasher."

"Thanks," I said, "I should probably head home soon."

I cleared my throat to clear all the questions I so wanted to ask.

He was wearing his grey cable cardigan now. With his hands deep in his sweater pockets his eyes rested on the photo of James Allen behind me, and then back to me he watched me prepare his tea.

"Say when," I said.

"Two's fine, thank you."

He reached over for the mug, and I handed it to him with the spoon.

His once huge, meaty hands were now more like my grandmother's: thinner, with veins visible.

I need air.

"I should probably head out soon," I said.

"Can you sit with me while I have my tea?"

"Of course," I said, and followed him back into his living room.

"How about some music?"

"Sure," I said, "what would you like to listen to?"

I got up and walked over to the other side of the room where he kept his albums in stacked wooden crates.

Albums with spines vertical, horizontal and some even resting on the diagonal. All randomly stored as if they had been packed, and moved, and listened to, and packed and moved again.

"Look for Supertramp," he said, "The *Breakfast in America* album."

I looked for what seemed a long time. The albums were all out of order much like his books were.

I wanted to organize his books and albums for him.

I wanted to scrub his kitchen.

"It should be on top shelf, towards the middle," he directed me.

"Side A" he said, "*Gone Hollywood.*"

I set the needle down gently and returned to the chair next to him.

"Turn it up," he said.

I got up and turned the volume knob up a few notches.

"I have never heard this album," I said.

I kept the paper sleeve out, and read the lyrics as we listened.

Mr. McG with his tea resting on his now concave belly reclined in his Lazy Boy.

Eyes closed, lost in reverie, his lips moved silently with the lyrics.

He asked me to re-set the needle and play that same song until the daylight was all gone from between the curtains, and the blue light of a dim streetlamp took its place.

I knew I had to get home soon or mom and dad would be sure to worry.

Since I got my license, mom had been so generous lending me her car for my voice lessons, and after-school activities when I asked.

I turned down the volume so I would not have to shout.

He opened his eyes, and for just a second I saw a flash of his face the way it was before. As if the music transported his visage back in time.

"I should head home," I said.

"OK, please take this," he said.

I walked his mug back to the kitchen, and washed it along with the spoon.

Even his dish drainer looked broken. It was a wooden one, cracked and stained.

Walking back out towards him I pointed to the stereo.

"Should I leave this on?"

"No, please turn it off now. I played it for you."

"Me?"

"Yes."

"Oh."

I put the record back exactly how I found it.

"Thank you for coming by," he said.

Mr. McG seemed like a shy little boy, picking at

the frayed cloth on the arm of his recliner.

"Should I come back again this week?" I asked.

"You want to hear the rest of that album. Don't you?"

"Are you sure you don't want me to call someone else for you?"

"No, just your company would be fine."

Finally my discomfort pushed the words up and out, and my mouth could not stop them.

"Why me?"

"What?"

"With all due respect, you haven't seen me for two years, you disappeared and now you ask for *me* to visit you? Why? I was your student...how can I help you?"

"Yes. That's right, Hope. I have not seen you for two years, but you are wrong about something. You *do know* how to help me."

"I'm sorry," I said falling over my words, "I don't want to upset you, but I just don't know what I can do. I want to help. I don't know how."

I stopped rambling, and stood still in the darkened room.

Mr. McG stood up slowly, and walked a few feet to the wall switch to turn on the light. He walked back to his chair and slumped down; he sighed a deep sigh, and then said,

"You always want to put things in order don't you?"

Silence.

It was true.

I wanted to organize and clean everything around him. Everything in that apartment. The overhead light exposed just how much work needed to be done.

I wanted to clean and organize that illness right out of his life.

"I don't know what to tell my parents," I said, "I don't know if my mom would approve of me being here. Alone with you."

I thought of when the first news of it broke, how mom read an article from the *New York Times* out loud.

"That's right you don't lie either do you? So you will have to figure that out."

He continued,

"Tell your mother where you are, and don't come to see me. Or come to see me, and don't tell her where you are. You have to make a choice."

Are those my only choices?

My face got hot and my feet even colder. For a moment I imagined how I hoped she would react.

I would tell mom Mr. McG was sick, and she would remember how much I liked him as a teacher. She would be concerned for him, and pleased that I wanted to help him. I imagined mom would ask me to wish him well from her, and make Chicken Soup and Toll House cookies to take along on my next visit. That's what she did when people at church were sick. Why would this be any different?

Mr. McG's directness and stare reminded me of

that first day of school when he grilled me about my name.

Then I remembered what she did say.

It's God's wrath.

Those are the words mom said after reading the article that past summer. Surely she would not want me to help him. Anyone else who was in need, yes, but this was different.

This had everyone scared.

Scared and ignorant in their fear.

I stared at a piece of popcorn on the rug, and could not help but pick it up. I pressed it between my thumb and forefinger.

Finally Mr. McG said,

"Well I think, that if you can come back and visit me again, Miss Hope Elizabeth Lawrence, I would very much like that, and your questions will all be answered. In time."

"OK," I said, "I will."

Of course I would return. I felt intimidated and drawn to this man just as I had two years before, and now he needed someone, and for whatever reason, he chose me.

"How about Thursday, after school. Would that work?"

"I shall look forward to it, Hope."

Driving home on the dark, cold, snowy roads back to my parent's house, I could not get the lyrics from *Gone Hollywood* out my head. The image of Mr. McG silently mouthing the words to

Gone Hollywood over and over. Frail, bony arms drumming along to the song; his body disappearing into that ugly Lazy Boy chair.

My tears came up and I let them go. Alone in the car on a dark road, it was safe to cry.

What had happened to him? What was this sudden cancer that was killing homosexuals? It ravaged him in such a short time.

How much we can change in an instant.

I knew that much.

Whether slow or fast we are all hurtling towards the inevitable.

Pitch, Yaw, and Roll.

Two and a half years since the move, and I still did not know how to navigate through life.

I still felt unmoored, responding to life as life came at me with no instruments to tell me if I was level or about to crash.

Now Mr. McG had asked for me.

Specifically, *me*.

I gripped the steering wheel, and clenched my jaw, willing my tears to stop.

I knew that whatever path Mr. McG asked me to walk down, I would do it because better than anything was the feeling of helping someone.

Mr. McG needed me, and helping him helped me to forget how lost I was, at least for an afternoon.

TOBY'S FIRST CHRISTMAS

Dad woke me at 5:00 am in the pitch dark of that last Monday before Christmas break. His morning whistle that I could never hear in our old house, I could always hear now in our tiny house in the woods where mom, dad and I lived on top of each other. Then again, maybe he never whistled in the mornings back in the city, because he was always stressed out. Now he was young again. Dad loved the mornings. Cheerfully knocking at my door,

"Beth? Time to get up."

"Yeah Dad, I'm up, I'm up," I said.

I pushed myself up and put my feet on the cold wood floor.

The woodstove made the second floor toasty. Dad always banked it at night, and he insisted I keep the electric heat in my bathroom and bedroom set to fifty degrees all winter. By morning, the air and floors were cold. I showered, dressed and could smell the coffee.

* * *

My caffeine addiction started early - in Sophomore year. I drank coffee to stay awake and cram for a French test.

French had been so easy that I never had to study, but my teacher made me memorize an entire section from Larousse, and I had to recite it for a grade. He said he would grade me on my pronunciation.

My accent was fine, but I had procrastinated committing it to memory.

The more bored I became with school, the more I put it off.

I had joined choir and loved that, but my studies were not engaging.

I was still coasting on the knowledge from my private school eighth grade education.

Besides what I learned in Freshman English from Mr. McG, Drivers Ed and Typing were the most valuable classes I had so far.

It was a slow decline that while in it, I did not see it. As a family we still had not discussed dad's retirement, the move or Eric's sudden death.

Stoic New England silence around sensitive emotional topics was a hallmark of our family. And I was too sensitive.

Any discipline that I had around my studies first grade through eighth was wearing away and crumbling beneath me.

So last December, when I stayed up cramming for a test, that was the night I discovered the magic of caffeine and would drink coffee for years to come.

* * *

Dad looked extra cheery this morning. He sat at the table with me and sipped his juice and coffee.

Mom was still in bed, snuggled under the blankets. They kept their bedroom even colder leaving the window open, mom insisted that "fresh air at night is good for you."

"What's on the docket today," Dad asked.

I yawned.

"I don't know," I said.

He looked over at my bookbag on the floor.

"Do you have any tests this week?"

"Yes," I said.

I looked at him and thought I would try one more time.

"Dad, can't I go back to my old school? They have boarding there. Lydia and William and George all got to go to private school. I miss it. I miss my friends. I miss my teachers and gymnastics and French and Latin. Pleeease?"

My voice trailed off.

I took one bite of my whole wheat toast with margarine, and it disgusted me. My stomach hurt again. I lost my appetite. Dad reached out and put his hand over mine and said,

"You're still studying French now aren't you? The teacher was kind enough to make time for you beyond Senior French. Now, wasn't that nice of him? You owe it to him to respect his time. The world is your oyster. You get out of it what you put into it."

Doubt.

There it was.

The doubt.

I believed he was right.

It was my fault.

Mea Culpa, Mea Culpa, Mea Maxima Culpa.

So what if I was bored, I could study harder.

I had tested into Senior French my freshman year and for this year and last, the teacher had worked with me twice a week for "independent" study, but it was awful. Every time I met him for my "class" he would pick at his bloody cuticles with his shaking hands and wave me on with "Bien, bien."

"Can I study French at Dartmouth next year? I can't get any more out of it than I already am. I want to continue studying languages. Please, can't we do something?"

He removed his hand from mine and said in a

calm, even serious tone,

"Beth, you have food on the table and a roof over your head. That is a lot more than most kids in this state have at your age."

I got up to get more coffee and brought the percolator over and filled his cup.

He smiled and said, "Thank you."

My stomach hurt still, and the margarine on my toast looked even more gross than before.

"Speaking of other families, it's that time again to do the Turkey Dinner Distribution this Sunday. I assume I can count on your help this time?"

"Yes," I said, and sat down pouting, "of course I'll help."

* * *

I dreaded those deliveries. Especially Tommy's house. Last year he tried to give me a bottle of vodka when I gave him the turkey.

"We can't accept any gifts," I'd said.

His eyes looked over my shoulder where my dad had parked up the driveway.

"No silly," Tommy said, "it's for you! You know, make that Christmas OJ a little brighter."

"For me? No. I don't drink."

He winked at me with a big smile on his face. One of his front teeth was chipped and grey.

"Right. I heard that," he said, "I was hoping it changed. After all, you're older now."

"Merry Christmas, and thank you but no," I

said.

He was beaming at me with his big broken smile, I felt my face getting hot.

You are not any better than him and shame on you for thinking you are.

I turned and walked away.

He laughed and said in a loud whisper at my back,

"Merry Christmas, and don't be mad when I try again next year."

When I got in the car, dad noticed something had happened.

I told him,

"Tommy wanted to give us a bottle of booze."

"Was it scotch?"

"What? No," I said, "vodka, and you told me to not accept any gifts when we are delivering turkeys. Right?"

"That's right, you did the right thing," he said, and patted my leg as we drove down the driveway toward the main road.

I had no desire to look back to see if he was watching.

I feared Tommy and that broken smile he always gave me now.

I feared what he saw in me that I didn't.

❋ ❋ ❋

Now it was another year later, and time for another church Turkey Delivery.

I had been excused at the Thanksgiving distribution this year because I had a terrible cold. Mom said it was my fault I got sick since I left the house with wet hair on a cold morning. So I had to help dad with the Christmas deliveries.

"So this Sunday, will you go to church with your mother and me? Then we can drop her back home, and deliver the turkey dinners."

"Sure dad," I said.

Be grateful you have a roof over your head and food on the table.

He smiled at me, his blue eyes cheerful again.

"Good, it's settled then. Your mother will be pleased."

He looked at his watch and said,

"Time to get you down to the bus. Oh and I almost forgot to tell you, the Pembertons will be arriving this weekend! Perhaps Toby would join us on Sunday?"

"The Pembertons? Really? This weekend?"

"Yes, they will stay though the second week of January, and their daughter will be joining them here for New Years."

My smile got much bigger, but quickly the doubt and worry crept back in, *why had Toby not written me that he was coming for Christmas?*

I had not heard from Toby for months, and my worries and sadness had been softened by my focus on Mr. McG and dad telling me several times: *I'm sure Toby is just very busy. Try not to worry.*

But I put that out of my mind because now, now today was wonderful, and the rest of the week would be wonderful.

Suddenly school was no longer boring, the snow was not as deep or cold and the blue grey light of morning looked lovely.

And what would he want for Christmas? I had presents to buy and cookies to bake. Would he ski with me?

Now that I had my license, I could drive us! We could go to Baker library alone and the bookstore and walk the snowy streets at twilight together and drink cocoa and maybe even have dinner at that cozy restaurant with the fireplace. Maybe we could even visit Mr. McG together. That is if Mr. McG was up to it. I wanted Toby to meet Mr. McG and I would just listen to them muse about great books.

Just the thought of Toby's arrival made my whole world brighter than it was before dad told me. I couldn't wait.

At school that morning Patty smiled at me because she knew me well enough that I did not smile hardly ever before first period.

"Well, don't you look like the cat who swallowed the canary," she said and pushed into my shoulder as we walked down the hall to class.

I teased her and said, "C'mon Patty you know I'm a dog person."

"What? You're not going to tell me. I will find out. You know I will."

By Saturday, I was so excited for Toby's arrival, our tiny house seemed even more suffocating than usual, and I decided to get my energy out on the slopes.

The T-lift was not operational, so I skied down and walked up with my skis slung over my shoulder. I had the whole mountain to myself.

To ski down took less than five minutes and over thirty to walk back up wearing my heavy ski boots.

By the second run, the warm feeling of good exercise began to melt my muscles. Too hot, I took off my short ski jacket and tied it around my waist.

My corduroy calves were caked in snow, and my sweat had soaked through my shirt and wool sweater.

I was feeling happy until halfway up the mountain I looked up and saw the afternoon shadows from the birch trees stretching long and wondered if what I had done was such a smart thing. Once the sun went down, it got cold fast.

Mom and dad were out Christmas shopping when I left the house, and I was the only one on the mountain.

Don't panic. Just keep going.

I had to side-step up the hill in the steeper parts as my legs began to shake from trudging straight up on the toes of my boots.

The sun was moving faster than I was, and

I could see my breath in the fading afternoon light. At least I had worn a hat this time. *I'll be alright.* I kept my eyes down to watch my boot placement. Falling with skis over one shoulder and poles in my right hand would be bad.

My focus became a moving meditation: *in breath, step, step; out breath, step, step.*

I rounded the last turn and looked up again.

Someone was standing at the top of the T-lift landing.

A wave.

Now the figure was coming towards me.

Toby? Was it Toby?

The snow was deep and not groomed.

When he fell down, I recognized his laughter and his loud cry,

"Bollocks!!"

Laughing, I yelled up to him,

"Maybe just try rolling down. Like a barrel."

I knew that could work because Patty and I had done that more than one time last winter. First by accident, and then for fun.

At first he tried to jog a bit, then fell, then rolled again and then stood up.

"Well that's just madness, thank you for that *terrible* suggestion," he yelled.

He turned and began to walk back up several steps, then stopped. He was covered in snow.

The sky was that perfect shade of blue right before the sun drops behind the mountain.

I kept trudging up at a faster pace now with

my boots straight-on into the hill again instead of side stepping.

My heart was bashing along joyfully with sweat pouring off my face. Any colder and it would freeze on my skin. Generally, I hated that. But right now the cold didn't seem to matter.

Only getting up to Toby mattered. Reaching for him.

When I was close enough to see his face he said to me,

"Are you mad?!"

"What," I said, "I've done this before."

"You're mad!"

He laughed and reached out to relieve me of my heavy skis and poles.

The wind was cutting through me now, icing the sweat between my breasts. I was getting chilled.

I put my jacket on and stepped closer to him.

He seemed even taller. He had grown, and he stood on the flat while I had just stopped short of the very top to put on my jacket.

He put my skis and poles down, and I thought he was going to hug me, but instead he unbuttoned his coat and reached inside.

He pulled out a silver flask and held it out to me.

"Here," he said, "this will warm you up."

"What is it?"

"My father's brandy, the one you liked."

My body had a craving for grapefruit juice.

A specific and definite craving.

I must have grapefruit juice.

"No thank you," I said, "I must get home and get out of these wet clothes."

He took off a glove with his teeth, unscrewed the top and put it to his lips.

I turned away from him and looked at the hill I had skied down, and the mountain range beyond it.

It was so beautiful.

I hated the isolation of this place, but sometimes I could not escape the truth of her beauty.

And the vast quiet. It was so, very, quiet.

I closed my eyes.

Sweat chilled on my face and scalp under my hat.

A slight wind.

The smell of snow.

The sound of Toby's "ahh" and then metal on metal, as he returned the silver cap to its flask.

I felt alive, vibrant.

Every part of my body was filled with energy and a peaceful calm at the same time.

Every sense awakened.

I turned back to look at him. He had one hand holding his coat open, and with his other hand he offered me his silver flask again.

"You sure?"

"I'm sure," I said, "thank you."

I watched as Toby returned the flask to the inside pocket of his long winter coat and buttoned up the front.

The sun was going down quickly.

If mom and dad were home, dad would be preparing his evening cocktail; he would be whistling along cheerfully to the sound of clanking bottles and ice.

In that moment I had a sadness in my heart that Toby was not the same boy I sat next to listening to his mother play Chopin two summers ago.

He was different.

And I was changing too.

Something unspoken between us.

Something must have happened to him in France.

He never carried a flask before.

I wanted to ask him so many questions.

Ophelia's Dilemma.

Mr. McG had shown me how to just be there.

Just be there.

And wait.

But I wanted to know. To know everything about his time in Italy; his family attending The Royal Wedding of Prince Charles and Lady Diana Spencer; his studies and adventures at school. He had been consistent in his letter writing, and then it just stopped.

Whatever time had passed between us since we had seen each other, I always imagined that his life was ten times bigger, better and grander than mine could ever be.

He put his hands on my shoulders, and smiled at me.

He was brighter now; the drink had warmed his face and mood.

He let go of my shoulders, and bent down and picked up his glove that had fallen on the ground. He put it on, and lifted my skis with one hand and handed me the poles.

He hoisted the skis on his shoulder as if they weighed nothing.

"Ok, then," he said, "let's crack-on and get you home."

I imagined this was how he always handled his skis.

Deftly, as if they were light as a feather. As if he'd done it a thousand times in the glorious sunshine of the Italian Alps.

On Christmas Eve, Toby joined us for the Christmas Eve service. He had asked his parents' permission, and they said he could go as long as he still attended Mass with them on Christmas Day.

I loved Christmas Eve service.

Toby had been to Anglican and Catholic Masses but never a Protestant Service.

When his parents said he could go, he had looked at me and winked saying,

"I guess I'm a blasphemer now, a heretic."

And he seemed to enjoy the idea of that.

I did not know the difference between Protestant and Catholic churches except for what Toby had told me, and this whole idea of purgatory that I read in Dante's *Divine Comedy*. I didn't know much about God or religion at all. It was all *feeling* without much knowledge. I loved Christmas and I knew Christmas was when we celebrated the birth of Jesus. And I knew there were three wisemen who brought him gifts because I had played one of them in the sixth grade play at my old school.

We all piled in Dad's Jeep Grand Wagoneer and headed to the little white steepled church in a small town nearby.

Getting out of the car, Toby smiled and said, "It's beautiful, just like a Norman Rockwell painting."

On the way into the church, we were each handed a candle and program.

My mother sat on the seat closest to the aisle, and I sat between my father and Toby.

Toby sang every song following along in the hymnal. At one point, during the signing of *Joy To The World*, he and my father became competing tenors, louder and louder.

I turned to him after that and whispered, "Are you glad you came with us?"

"Yes," he said, "I'm chuffed to be with you and experience this."

At the end of the service, the first candle is lit as a lone voice begins to sing *Silent Night*, then voices join in one by one as the light is shared one person to the next.

❊ ❊ ❊

The lighting of candles and singing took me back to Christmas Vespers at my old school. Specifically to when I was in first grade, and my sister was in twelfth.

Grades first through eleventh sat in the darkened auditorium in solemn, silence anticipating the beginning of Christmas Vespers.

The doors opened, and the Senior girls entered two abreast, holding candles and singing the old song *Masters In This Hall*.

I looked for her, then there she was: Lydia, my sister, holding her candle, singing,

> *Nowell! Nowell! Nowell!*
> *Nowell! Sing we clear!*

I looked up at her and felt so proud; felt so much love for her. *There's my sister!*

Paige was sitting next to me, and we both waved and sang ebulliently. Lydia quickly smiled at us her face beautifully lit by candlelight, and they walked on to where the seniors sat every Christmas.

I so looked forward to being a Senior like Lydia, and to walk in holding a candle singing that song. I loved the annual tradition of Vespers at my old school; annually marking time, each grade sat in a specific area of the auditorium, and did specific things each year.

I never got to walk in as a senior holding a candle singing *Masters In This Hall*.

❈ ❈ ❈

When I tipped my candle flame to light Toby's candle, he looked me right in my eyes. He saw my tears, and smiled that same kind smile I saw that summer we met. It was deeper now, richer and more real in the eyes.

We walked out of the church all singing *Silent Night* holding our candles.

Once outside, we blew them out and then had brief chit-chat where my mom and dad introduced Toby to their friends as "our neighbor from across the pond."

On the way home, my heart was full to bursting.

Mom turned around from the front passenger seat. She was happy too, and had that smile I saw so rarely.

"What did you think Toby," she asked.

"Grand, just grand," he said, "far more joyful than all that up and down and up and down and kneeling that I will have to do tomorrow!"

Dad looked back in the rear view mirror at us, "So you enjoyed it then?"

"Yes," Toby said.

He placed his gloved hand on my mittened one

and said to my parents,

"I quite enjoyed it. Very much. Thank you."

"Join us for a nightcap before you head back home, Toby?"

Mom cut in with, "Or cocoa. How about I make you kids some hot cocoa. From scratch."

"That sounds great mom," I said.

"Yes, thank you," Toby said. He looked over at me and squeezed my mittened hand.

When we walked into the house mom and dad put their candles on the kitchen counter. I picked them up and left my mittens in their place.

"I will start the cocoa," mom said.

She seemed happy to have a task to do. And she cheerfully added, "I can even make us homemade whipped cream. We will let you kids know when it's ready."

"Mom makes the best hot cocoa and whipped cream anywhere," I said to Toby, "come with me, and bring your candle please. You don't have to, but if you want to."

Toby followed me out into our back yard. The deep snow was soft and it sparkled under the clear starlit sky.

"What are you doing?"

"You'll see."

I knelt down and began to bank the snow in a small circle to protect from wind. I placed our three candles in the snow.

The back door opened behind me.

"You may want these," dad said, and he handed

Toby a small box of wooden matches.

"Thanks daddy," I said as he went back into the house.

Toby knelt down in his thick coat across from me. I straightened the three candles in the snow, and then asked him,

"Would you like to include your candle with ours?"

"You must be Catholic; this is downright pagan! I love it. Yes, yes, you may have my candle."

He handed me his candle, and I placed it in the snow with my bare hands.

Toby handed me the box of small wooden matches, and I lit each candle and blew out the match.

I prayed aloud the Our Father Prayer and gave thanks for mom and dad and went through my prayers for the whole family (even George). I prayed my special Christmas prayer and thanked God for Toby joining us this Christmas Eve. Amen.

Toby stared at the small flames from the small white candles in the snow. The snow around them glowed golden.

"Thank you," he said his voice a husky whisper of emotion, "I...I am very glad you invited me. It's so different than what I am used to. Very different."

He looked away towards the darkness at the edge of our yard.

"When I was in Italy," his voice started to crack.

He cleared his throat, and said, "When I was in Italy - I spent some time... And I... When I..." he sighed a big sigh and looked at me.

His eyes shined in the candlelight.

Toby removed his hat, his blond hair longer and more flaxen than I had remembered. His hair reminded me of Paige from so many years before.

My funny valentine.

"I am so sorry I did not write you back," he said, "I should have written you...like we'd promised."

"That's alright," I said, "I know you were very busy."

He raised his hand, "No, that's not. Not alright. Sorry, but that's not it."

"Ok," I said.

Waiting.

I closed my eyes and prayed again. The stars felt closer that night. I listened.

Just wait. Now is NOT the time to ask him any questions.

I opened my eyes. He looked down at his gloved hands and with a flash he clapped them together twice. Hard, with a violence, and then pressed them to his forehead.

"Dammit," he said, "you are the only one I can talk to. Now I can't even talk to you."

He took off his gloves and reached into his coat pocket. I thought he was getting his handkerchief, but he pulled out that silver flask, un-screwed it and took a long pull.

Just as he slipped it back in his pocket, the door opened.

"Cocoa will be ready in just a minute. Good-ness! It's cold out here," mom said, and quickly shut the door.

I panicked wondering if mom saw Toby drink from his flask.

My fingers were numb and looked red even in candlelight. I wanted my mittens that were in-side on the kitchen counter, but I did not move.

I waited for Toby to tell me. I would wait as long as he needed me to.

Toby lifted his head, and looked me right in my eyes.

Now with liquid courage he said,

"A priest - "

He took a deep breath through his nose, ex-haled and said,

"A priest..."

The light went out of his eyes when he said it. His mouth thinned; his face changed. Frighten-ing. It wasn't Toby's face I knew looking at me.

"...a priest raped me."

The door behind us opened with mom's voice again.

"OK, you two, get in here, it's cold and cocoa is on the table!"

The door closed.

My body froze.

"My God, Toby, that's..."

I wanted to hug him, to comfort him, but I could not move.

"I don't know what to say. That's so dreadful, awful."

"Exactly," he said looking down at the candles burning between us, "quite. Horrid. Underground, in a crypt - on the altar. Bloody sacrafice!! God, God. God??? What is...who is God?"

His voice cracked, his words broken now, and a bit louder he spit out,

"A priest is supposed to be *In Persona Christi*. He stands in the place of *Christ* and he..."

Toby started to weep, and then he gasped; breathing-in his tears and snot like a death rattle. His face shining wet with horrible pain and his effort to fight it.

"It hurt like hell. That bloody bastard."

He looked down and exhaled with control, slowing his breath.

"I am glad you're here, you are the only person I can talk to. Who will believe me? A priest?!" he said.

"I believe you," I said quietly.

"I so wanted to tell you, but I couldn't even write it down. *Bloody awful.* And I couldn't write to you without telling you. So I didn't write to you after it happened."

The door opened again.

"Everything ok out here," Dad asked.

"Yes, dad, we'll be right there," I yelled back

over my shoulder.

I knew they could see us. The kitchen windows looked right out on the backyard.

Toby reached into his coat pocket again, this time pulling out a white handkerchief.

He wiped his face and put his hat back on.

My heart broke open for him. I wanted to help, to take his pain, I felt it sharp in my heart, and I was crying too.

"What can I do, Toby, my God, what can I do? Please tell me."

He inhaled deeply again, his real face was back now, and the frightening one I saw for only a second had vanished.

Then he said,

"I don't know if I can even believe in God anymore. Why would God let that happen?"

He looked up at the sky, then down at the candles, then at me and said,

"But tonight, I felt something. Something real and good. Will you...will you please pray for me?"

"Yes," I said, "absolutely."

And I prayed right there for Toby. Under the stars, out loud, on the cold snow by the candles that were still burning a soft golden light between us.

Then we got up, I hugged him, and we went inside.

Dad knew something was up, his face showed concern as he took Toby's coat, hat and scarf and hung them on a chair by the woodstove.

Dad looked directly at Toby and said,

"Toby, I am so glad you joined us tonight. It's a tradition for us to open one present on Christmas eve. Would you join us while you have your cocoa?"

"Thank you Mr. Lawrence," he said, "you are very kind."

Mom brought over a side table for Toby and we all sat around the tree with cocoa and cookies.

I was still stunned from what Toby had told me, like my body was there and not there.

We gathered around the tree, and the warmth of my mug of hot cocoa began to warm my hands. The tree was beautiful. The fire in the woodstove, orange flames and the occasional hissing and popping sounds of wet hardwood damp from the snow. I was happy that dad invited Toby to join us, and the happiness melted away the tide of darkness that had risen a few minutes before.

"Please, permit me," dad said to us, and he reached for a present I had not seen before that was far back under the tree.

"Merry Christmas," he said, and handed it to Toby. My mom was smiling and had whipped cream on her top lip from the cocoa.

Dad proceeded to hand me a present and then mom, and finally, he took one for himself.

"We open them one at a time," I said, "guests go first."

"Oh, alright," Toby said.

He pulled the ribbon and slowly opened the paper taking care to not tear it.

"I hope it's not scotch," mom said, her tone half joking and half serious.

Toby opened the box and unfolded the red and white tissue paper inside.

"What is it, c'mon," I said, unable to hide my curiosity.

Toby lifted out a lovely plaid wool blue scarf. He wrapped the scarf around his neck, the blue made his eyes look bright again.

"Thank you, Mr. and Mrs. Lawrence."

He put his hand up to his neck.

"It's warm, just lovely, thank you."

He looked down at the box still in his lap, and lifted more tissue paper,

"Oh, and what, a book?"

"What is it," mom asked wiping her mouth with a red Christmas napkin.

It was clear that my dad had prepared this present alone although the tag read from "The Lawrence Family".

Toby slowly lifted out a thick leather book with gilded edges.

Dad looked at my mother anticipating her question when he said,

"Toby I did check with your father, and he said it was just fine to give this to you."

I was still in the dark, I did not know what book it was.

Toby opened it carefully as if opening a jeweled box of treasure.

"It's the 1611 version of the King James Bible," Toby said.

"I know you have missals and masses and lots of prayer and tradition," dad said, "Beth told us how much you love reading classic books. This is a good classic to read too."

In that moment I was happy for Toby, but I also felt a sting of sadness.

Mom and dad had never given me a Bible. I had stopped going to church every week with them, but I still wondered why they gave him such a lovely Bible, when they had never given me one. Not even when I was younger.

Don't be so selfish. This is a lovely thing dad has done for Toby.

Toby silently turned the pages, then closed it carefully, set the box down and reached over to shake my dad's hand,

"Thank you, sir. Really, this means so much to me."

He paused and then said,

"I really enjoyed the service tonight, it was so different than what I am used to, and it was...." his voice trailed off into silence.

Then just before things got too awkward, mom chimed in,

"Well, I will open mine next!"

It was a smaller box, and I knew what it was since dad gave her the same size box every Christmas eve; and every year she was just as genuinely pleased as the last.

He always gave her customized Crane stationary with her initials embossed in script at the top.

It was lovely.

The envelopes were lined with the same color as the border of the paper.

She loved writing letters and thank you notes, and went through a box or more every year.

She kissed my dad.

"Thank you, my darling. I love the color you chose for me this year."

She sat back down in her rocking chair and smiled at dad again. Their love was decades old now, and still so real. Love like that was much rarer than I knew.

We finished our Christmas Eve tradition of opening one gift, and sipped our cocoa until dad looked at his watch and said,

"Well, we'd better all hit the hay. We don't want to be awake when Santa comes down that stove pipe!"

Dad was so silly, I laughed half loving his dry humor, and half embarrassed for his dry humor.

"I will walk you out," I said to Toby.

Toby held my hand as we walked down my driveway and down the road a few feet to the edge of his.

The sky seemed even brighter than before every star reflecting off the thick, white snow. The world seemed bigger. The air cold and dry.

The silence of the night broken only by the sound of crunching snow under our feet and all the words spoken and unspoken.

His blue eyes alive and smiling. My brown ones smiling back at him.

"Merry Christmas, Tobias Oliver Pemberton," I whispered.

He stepped even closer to me, and said,

"Merry Christmas, Hope Elizabeth Lawrence."

We stood like that for a long time. Just looking into each other. Reaching for what we knew was our past, present and future.

And then, just like that.

Toby kissed me.

. . .

End of Volume 1

DISCUSSION QUESTIONS

1. What were the most significant imprints from Beth's childhood?

2. How do you think these emotional imprints from childhood shaped her personality, and how might they impact her future?

3. Do Beth's teenage imprints add to, magnify or change the ones she has already from childhood?

4. Discuss her relationship with Toby. How do her emotional imprints shape it? What new imprints will form?

5. Do you think Beth returned to visit Mr. McG? If so, what do you think she told her mother? What would you do in that scenario?

6. What do you think the title of the book means? Who is *Dorian's Quarterback*?

7. What character(s) can you most relate to and/ or least relate to?

EMOTIONAL IMPRINTS SERIES
Explores questions such as: Are one's emotional imprints knowable? Can a person change the course of their life, or will they be forever sub-consciously chained to their imprints of the past?

Dorian's Quarterback - A Novel

Beth Lawrence's emotional imprint journey from her 1970s childhood through 1981 when she is sixteen and falls for Toby.

Dinosaurs & Snow Angels

Some early childhood imprints.

Pitch, Yaw & Roll

Beth struggles to orient herself in an unfamiliar world.

The Grand Fascination

Beth continues to grow and meet new chal-lenges.

PRAISE FOR DORIAN'S QUARTERBACK

"An affecting Proustian realist novel about childhood emotional development, Mary Taylor's Dorian's Quarterback is an accomplished rumination on the impact of sense memories and the nature of time. Following a young girl named Beth growing up in a privileged New England family in the 1970s, the novel tackles subjects like mental illness, teen suicide, and homophobia with genuine nuance and confident, intimate prose. The cover doesn't nearly reflect the artistry inside, as author Taylor paints an arresting portrait of a girl coming of age in the midst of family crisis."

Self-Publishing Review, ★ ★ ★ ★
January, 2022

PRAISE FOR DINOSAURS
& SNOW ANGELS

"A series of snapshot vignettes that weave into an immersive "novelloir," Dinosaurs & Snow Angels by Mary Taylor is a non-traditional story of the watershed moments that mark every family and life. Capturing nuanced identities in a single turn of phrase or offhand comment and pulling readers into the intimate scenes that define a young girl's perspective, this book is a visceral ode to childhood, sisterhood, and the silent struggles of youth. Easing readers in with a conversational narration, the author also delivers striking strings of language throughout this unique and revealing read."

Self-Publishing Review, ★ ★ ★ ★

PRAISE FOR PITCH, YAW & ROLL

"A gut-punch of a read, told through the pained lens of a young girl desperately trying to find her place, Pitch, Yaw & Roll: Identity, Love & Addiction by Mary Taylor is an evocative and stirring YA drama. In the perennial effort to connect and fit in, young Beth is led down a variety of slippery slopes, teetering between teenage rebellion, personal discovery, and dangerous compromises to her still-forming values. Challenging as this read may be for readers who can relate, the authentic dialogue, visceral self-reflection, and unflinching narrative voice make this a straightforward, but hard-hitting tale that has a lasting impact."

Self-Publishing Review, ★ ★ ★ ★

ACKNOWLEDGEMENTS

Although a writer spends hour upon hour and day after day alone, a writer is never truly alone. Haunted by ghosts, loved by angels, and cajoled by characters who appear on the page as if by magic, the writer finds home. Je suis, I am. This book would not be possible without the lessons and challenges of life's mentors and teachers, and the encouragement of many including my beloved mother and father. And to one in particular: I say, "Thank you 'my Hemingway', we did it." *Thank you for such an amazing year. I love you.*

ABOUT THE AUTHOR

Mary Taylor

 Artist Heart. Tech Brain. Author. Writing about the mystery of life and the adventures of human experience in all its complexity is a passion for me. Blackstone-finn.com

"She came to me a skillful writer, able to write a smart sentence, but now she has embodied Dangerous Writing and has developed a particular voice of her own." ~ Tom Spanbauer, Author, February 22, 2007

"Mary's style is unique as she captures deep raw emotions in a way that engages you as a reader, and helps you understand the fears and insecurities of this young girl trying to navigate life." ~ Shelley C. Wagner

"...I particularly enjoyed the author's writing style and her use of humor and emotion to tell this story." ~ Bill Wixted